Praise for K. A. Mitchell's *Diving In Deep*

"If you're in the mood for a read with two hot men, great love scenes, and lots of emotion, don't hesitate to pick up Diving in Deep, but be warned—you won't want to put it down!"

~ *Joyfully Reviewed*

"K.A. Mitchell has created an amazing tale of genuine emotions, humorous dialog and erotic love scenes..."

~ *Literary Nymphs*

"...hot with a capital H, I highly recommend you pick up Diving In Deep."

~ *Romance Reviews Today—Erotic*

Look for these titles by
K. A. Mitchell

Now Available:

Custom Ride
Hot Ticket
Regularly Scheduled Life
Collision Course

Print Anthologies
Temperature's Rising
Serving Love

Diving In Deep

K. A. Mitchell

A Samhain Publishing, Ltd. publication.

Samhain Publishing, Ltd.
577 Mulberry Street, Suite 1520
Macon, GA 31201
www.samhainpublishing.com

Diving In Deep
Copyright © 2009 by K. A. Mitchell
Print ISBN: 978-1-60504-090-5
Digital ISBN: 1-59998-896-8

Editing by Sasha Knight
Cover by Anne Cain

First Samhain Publishing, Ltd. electronic publication: March 2008
First Samhain Publishing, Ltd. print publication: January 2009

Dedication

For Casey, Rachel and Wendy who fell in love with them page by page.

Chapter One

"Is this room going to be all right?"

Cameron dragged out his bright Havers Safety Training Company smile, and turned to face Bill, the site coordinator for Bay County Community College. "It'll be great. The AV equipment's set, right?"

Bill gave a nod as Cameron looked past the forgettable Bill to the participants milling around the college classroom for the renewal course, an update on the latest water safety and rescue procedures. Forcing back a sigh of relief, Cameron hoisted the briefcase that barely made the cut-off for airline carry-ons onto the table at the front of the room.

He took a minute to assess the room and found it no better or worse than any of the dozens he'd been in or would be in this spring, his fourth as a national trainer. He'd worked damned hard to get here, he reminded himself, trying to stuff back the weird restlessness he'd probably picked up from being stuck freezing his ass off in Buffalo in mid-March. Today, if he finished up by two, he would be digging his toes in the sand of Panama City Beach. He loved his job.

Bill handed over the remote for the DVD, and Cameron opened his briefcase, sneaking a glance at the broad-shouldered back of the guy talking to a woman in the front row. Cameron had to fight the instinct to arch his brows in admiration. Checking out the trainees was regrettably frowned on by the Havers Safety Team. Cameron usually considered it one of the perks of his job, but he dragged himself into the sexual harassment seminars and signed off on the paperwork and didn't plan to get reprimanded for eyeing a hot piece of Floridian ass. Though in Cameron's defense, he could mention Exhibit A: the man's broad shoulders that cut into Exhibit B: a narrow waist with Exhibit C: a lickable dip before the clincher, Exhibit D: that jean-clad, apple-shaped ass.

Suddenly Cameron couldn't wait until they moved to the pool section of the training. Florida sun, eye candy, yeah, this was shaping up to be quite an improvement over the Buffalo trip.

"Oh, someone here says he knows you," Bill said.

Cameron kept his happy-to-be-here smile fixed on his face. "That's possible. I grew up not far from here."

Bill went into the front row and reached up to tap on one of the shoulders that made up Cameron's air-tight defense. Someone had made a mistake. Cameron would have remembered a guy with that build, twelve years away from home or no.

Mr. Eyecandy turned around. Black hair fell forward over a pair of bright blue up-tilted eyes. The face was the same, a little stronger. The eyes still held that familiar burning energy. But the rest of him...there was no way he was looking at Adam's kid brother.

"Noah?"

Noah smiled. God, had he always had those dimples?

"Hey, Cam."

There was still a husky whisper when he spoke that nickname, like it was some kind of code they shared.

A code Cameron really would be better off forgetting.

∿∿

Semester break, junior year in college, and Cameron fought the weight of his eyelids as he squinted at music videos through the haze of a few too many beers. He was stretched out on the couch in Adam's basement while Adam drowned out the best parts of the songs with his snores from the recliner. Cameron wasn't exactly asleep, but he wasn't completely awake when he felt the press of a body on his, lips coaxing a kiss from his own before he surfaced.

He shoved at bony shoulders, forced himself up on his elbows. "Noah?" Cameron's eyes focused on his best friend's kid brother, all long bones and floppy hair.

"Cam."

That stupid nickname he'd dumped in college breathed right over his face from wide pink lips he'd tried never to look at, lips that were dropping down onto his. Cameron shoved harder.

Okay, so he'd noticed that Adam's little brother had a crush on him. The kid made it pretty damned obvious. Cameron had felt Noah's eyes on him a bit too long, and he'd thought it was kind of cute when Noah defied three generations of Braves fans to buy himself a Yankees hat like Cameron's. But this—God, if Adam tried something like this with Cameron's sixteen-year-old sister, he'd beat the shit out of him, friend since kindergarten or no.

The flickering TV light showed Noah's eyes, pleading and uncertain, with a sexy tilt Cameron had never seen before. Noah licked his lips, and Cameron needed the kid off his lap—

now.

But Noah was strong. "Cam," he whispered again.

"No," Cameron managed to choke out, willing the alcohol to keep a flare of interest from tenting his jeans.

"Why? I know. I know you're gay."

Cameron shot a look over at Adam, still snoring on the recliner, thank God. When Cameron had finally worked up the nerve to tell Adam last year, he had shrugged and muttered, "Whatever, dude. Not like it's that much of a shock." Cameron had a feeling that swapping saliva with Adam's kid brother didn't fall into the *whatever* category.

"He didn't tell me. I knew."

"And—"

"And I am, too."

"You're fifteen, Noah. I'm sure a lamppost is looking pretty good some days."

Noah didn't move but Cameron could see that hit, a bitchslap to his prickly fifteen-year-old ego.

"I've seen you look at me." Noah's tone was full of defiance.

An ego that was pretty quick to bounce back. And fuck if Noah didn't have Cameron there. It wasn't as if he actively spent time perving on Adam's baby brother but damn, when the kid passed gawky last year he got pretty. Bright eyes through that dark hair, tall, and he was just always around.

"Noah, get off."

"Why?"

"You're fifteen. It's illegal, man."

"I'll be sixteen in a few months."

"Your brother will kill me."

"He's been passed out for an hour." Noah shifted against

Cameron's crotch, breath hot and sticky against his neck, and holy fucking goddamn there was no hiding his erection now.

Noah grinned, his tongue pressing up against sharp white teeth, his eyes tilting even more, and Cameron clung to a last shred of control.

"Noah. Get off me. Now."

"But you—"

"Fucking hell, Noah." Cameron bucked the brat off right onto the floor and caught his breath. "I'm a guy. Sometimes it just happens."

Noah looked like Cameron had kicked him in the balls. Cameron started to reach out and run his hand through that mess of black hair, but jerked his hand back before he made contact. Cameron could remember being fifteen and confused and wanting so goddamned bad to know what all those mixed up feelings meant, but this wasn't going to happen. He'd known Noah all his life and—no. Cameron couldn't be that answer. Not for Noah.

At the next commercial, Noah shoved himself off the floor and thumped back upstairs. Cameron didn't see the kid the rest of the break.

〰
〰

Noah watched recognition slam into Cameron. It was pretty satisfying to see always cool and self-possessed Cameron Lewis gasping like a landed fish. Cam pulled himself back together with a visible effort.

"So how's Adam?"

"Great." Noah offered his hand and after an almost imperceptible hesitation Cam took it. "He and Maria have two

13

boys, a house, the whole works. They're over in Jacksonville now."

Was Cameron blushing? Was he thinking about Adam and Maria's wedding? The night after? Cam seemed to be trying to look everywhere but at him, and he pulled his hand free a little sooner than was polite.

"I've got to"—he jerked his chin at the room—"get things started."

"Yeah." Noah stepped back.

"Maybe we can talk after."

"I'm sure you've got other things to do."

Cameron's gaze snapped back to his face, surprise widening his green eyes.

Noah shrugged and hid a smile. "I just wanted to say hi." And he folded himself into a seat in the front row.

For a guy who wanted to get things started, Cam took an awfully long time organizing his materials and fiddling with the DVD player. Noah flipped through his handouts, glancing up through the tails of his bangs when Cam dropped a binder. He shouldn't take so much pleasure in upsetting Cam's equilibrium, but since he'd been doing it to Noah since he figured out what his dick was for, he thought Cam kind of deserved it.

When Cam finally faced the room and urged people to their seats, Noah could feel Cam's attention just from the number of times he didn't look Noah's way. As the DVD played through Spinal Injury Management, Noah caught the nervous drum of Cam's fingers against his hip where he leaned against the podium. The Cameron Noah knew had always been too confident to fidget, and Noah really hoped he was the reason. As soon as he'd seen Cameron's name pop up on the schedule, he'd been wondering how six years had changed the guy, how

14

Cam would react when he saw Noah again.

He'd stopped comparing other guys to Cam after that first year, but Noah couldn't say he'd forgotten him, forgotten that night—one scary and perfect night.

♒

Cam hadn't stopped drinking after the best man's toast, but they were both a lot less drunk than they were pretending when Noah followed Cam up to his hotel room after Adam's wedding reception. When Cam turned and looked at him in the hall, Noah didn't know what was making him sweat more, the way his heart pounded in his throat, the tangle of nerves in his stomach or the throb of his cock in his tuxedo pants.

Cam leaned against his door for a few minutes, just looking at him. He twisted the keycard through his fingers.

Noah's mouth went dry as he watched those long fingers twine around the card. "I turned nineteen last month."

"Don't remind me." Cameron swiped the key and opened his door.

Noah was pretty sure something in his head was going to explode as he waited.

"Come on in." Cam held the door open after he'd stepped inside.

He sounded more amused than horny, but Noah didn't care. He hurried through before Cam could change his mind.

All through the reception, Noah had tried to force some kind of recognition out of Cam, taking every opportunity to get next to him, brushing up against him in the limo—anything to convince Cam he wasn't just some kid anymore. Noah knew he'd gotten one or two appraising stares, knew he didn't look fifteen anymore, but every time he had thought Cameron would walk over and say something, Cam had turned and talked to someone else.

Finally, Noah had walked out of the ballroom and into the hotel bar. The bartender had given him a look, but since Noah hadn't tried to order anything, the guy hadn't chased him out. Not that Noah needed more to drink. Adam and their older cousins had been handing Noah drinks all night anyway. He'd watched a pool game for a few minutes until he felt someone next to him. He didn't have to look to know it was Cam. The hair on Noah's arms had stood up like he was picking up some kind of vibration in the air.

"So." Cam had breathed alcohol on Noah's face as he turned in Cam's direction.

Noah swallowed, then just stared. Anything he said could screw this up, and he couldn't, not now when Cameron was finally looking at him like Noah had something Cam wanted.

"Still think you're gay?" Cam whispered.

Noah laughed. "I know it." He'd straightened up. He'd grown another inch in college, and Cam had to look up at him.

"Hmm. We'll see." Cam winked before he stepped away, swaying a bit as he made his way out of the bar.

Now, Cam leaned against the wall in the small entry hall of his hotel room. Maybe he was too drunk. Noah felt a pang of guilt and turned back toward the door. Cam caught Noah's arm and pressed him into the opposite wall.

Then it was Cameron slamming into him, Cameron fucking Lewis grinding against him, eyes staring into Noah's with pupils so wide only a thin rim of green showed around the black. Noah's dick went from throbbing to aching.

"This what you're after, Noah?"

Noah couldn't speak so he just wrapped a hand around Cam's neck and hauled his head forward. Cam's lips parted in a smile against his, and as Noah's tongue slid inside, that wet rub went all the way down to his dick. He tightened his legs to hold himself up against the rush of blood flooding his cock.

Cam's mouth was sweet from champagne, and he laughed into Noah's kiss, hands tangling in Noah's jacket as Cam worked on the buttons. Giving up on the buttons, his hand pressed lower, rubbing Noah's cock through his trousers. The feel of Cam's hand on Noah's dick, even through the layers of clothing, had his head swimming, and he was going to come way too soon if he didn't do something now.

Noah grabbed Cam's lapels and shoved him backward across the hall. Cam was still laughing as his back hit the wall with a thud, laughed as Noah's tongue licked down Cam's neck. He stopped laughing when Noah dropped to his knees.

Noah clenched his fists to stop his hands from trembling before he reached for Cameron Lewis's fly. How many times had he done this in his fantasies? How many times in the last year had he sucked some guy at a party and wished it was Cam in his mouth, shooting thick and deep in his throat?

Panic pumped acid into Noah's stomach, and he knew he had to hurry before Cam changed his mind. Noah worked quickly, pulling him through his fly and wrapping his lips around Cam as soon as that perfect mushroom head cleared the cloth. Noah licked, teasing under the ridge, lapping the salty drops from the slit, and then sucked Cam in farther.

Cam's hand landed on Noah's hair, threaded through his bangs and lifted them back until Noah had to look up at him.

"Holy shit, Noah."

Noah had learned quite a bit about sucking cock his first year away from home, and he was planning on showing every trick to Cam. Noah relaxed his jaw, his throat, and took that thick cock so deep his lips kissed the slick surface of Cam's trousers.

"Nuhh—"

Whatever Cam was going to say got swallowed by the moan that broke from his lips. It might have been Noah's name, it might have been a protest, but Cam's hand just urged Noah closer, so he swallowed around the satiny pressure in his throat. After pulling back with a long teasing lick, Noah reached up to play with the soft sac still trapped in the silky fabric before sucking on the head once more.

Cam hissed through his teeth and then a loud thunk made Noah pull all the way off until the crown left his lips with a soft plop. Cam thumped his head against the wall while Noah watched.

"Fucking hell, Noah." Cam's lips were wide and wet, as if he'd been the one with a dick down his throat. He panted for a second then whispered, "Take me deep again. Please."

Noah licked around the head, tasted the come leaking from the slit before he screwed his lips down on the shaft, slow and tight and wet. Cam's fingers moved to Noah's cheek, thumb rubbing across his stretched lips and down inside the hollow of his cheek.

"Never...knew...ah...you'd grow up..."

Noah wrapped his hand around the base and increased the speed of his strokes.

"Shit...you'd grow up to be such a cocksucker."

Noah dropped his hand and opened his throat again, gulping Cam down and counting on his swimmer's lungs to keep him full of air as he sucked the last bit of amused arrogance out of the bastard.

With his hand tightening in Noah's hair, Cam tugged Noah off until his eyes watered.

"What?" Noah looked up at Cam's flushed face.

"I don't want to come yet."

Noah stretched his neck and licked the dark red head so close to his lips. "You can go again."

Cam made a sound like he was gargling chlorine and then jerked away. "At least let me get this tux off. I am not coming in another man's pants."

Noah reached to tug at the waistband, and Cam knocked Noah's hand away. He climbed to his feet.

"Be hard to get the deposit back if you come all over that." Cam nodded at Noah's own rented tuxedo.

It was like back diving off the highboard, trusting the water was going to be there when you finally arced down, a moment of panicked free fall while every muscle tensed. Noah bit his lip and unbuttoned his jacket. "You gonna make me?"

Cam's pants and jacket were already over a chair. He stepped up to shove the jacket off of Noah's shoulders. "Yeah."

Noah was free-falling again, and the water was a long way down.

Cam threw his jacket on the other chair and yanked Noah's shirt out of his pants. "You're gonna come so hard you'll forget where you are." Then he stepped away. "So get that off or get messy."

Noah was still working on his cummerbund when Cam ripped the covers off the king-sized bed and sat on the edge, leaning back on his arms. Noah's fingers fumbled even more because his brain shorted out at the sight of Cam naked on a bed, waiting for *him*. Fuck the deposit. Noah ripped the satin free.

Looking at the man on the bed, Noah almost drooled. Golden-brown skin everywhere but a small patch of white around his hips and thighs. Gold-flecked green eyes, dark blond curls with sun gold highlights. Light blond hair starting below his pecs, darkening beneath his navel as it trailed down to frame his cock. Noah was finally staring at Cameron Lewis's gorgeous cock, and he had to get it back in his mouth. Now.

It took two steps to drop between those gold-furred thighs and wrap his lips around the red, leaking crown. Cam's hand was back on Noah's head, petting him, urging him and Noah took a deep breath and swallowed that beautiful cock down until he almost had the whole length. Cam's moan didn't have a trace of smugness in it now. Noah pulled back and started bobbing, until Cam's hand lifted him off.

"I don't want to come like that." Cam reached under Noah's arm and dragged him onto the bed.

Noah was pretty sure he knew what Cam meant. And if Noah was honest with himself, wasn't this why he'd said "No thanks, not into that" all this past year because he was waiting, wishing it would be Cam?

Cam didn't leave any room for doubt because as soon as Noah was stretched out next to Cam, he licked under Noah's ear and murmured, "Want to come in your tight little ass."

Noah was pretty sure he must have passed out for a second because the next thing he knew Cam was wrapping his lips around Noah's cock, and it felt like the first time anyone had ever blown him, so hot and wet and *oh-God-oh-God there's a mouth on my dick*. He didn't know he could get that hard and not shoot. He was afraid if he touched Cam's head Noah would do something stupid like rip out Cam's hair so Noah just fisted his hands on his thighs and tried not to buck up into that bone-melting heat. Cam backed off long enough to suck on

Noah's sac, mouthing one side and then the other before licking underneath. Noah's whole body shook with the effort to stay still.

"Roll over."

Noah didn't think there were two sexier or scarier words in the English language, especially not when Cameron was growling them.

He twisted and rolled, his heart slamming high and tight in his chest. Cam stroked his hands down Noah's ass to his thighs before sliding back up to pull his cheeks apart. He didn't realize he was holding his breath until Cam licked *there* and then Noah couldn't breathe at all.

Cam's hot tongue worked around the entrance to Noah's body, flicking, wetting, while his hands pulled him wider, fingers digging in hard. Noah squirmed, and Cam held Noah tighter, spread him wide open for the hot pressure of a tongue spearing inside.

"Oh. God." It was all Noah could manage to say.

Cam's laugh was warm and deep, vibrating against that sensitive skin. Then he was licking again, tongue flicking about a million tiny nerve endings, and Noah groaned until his throat hurt. When Cam drove his tongue in and sucked, Noah couldn't help it; he bucked back into that blinding heat and pleasure.

Cam's mouth lifted away, and a finger pressed against that throbbing opening. "What's the matter, Noah, can't find any college boys to eat your ass?"

Noah groaned as Cam's finger slid inside. Noah had gotten this far, had let a guy finger him while blowing him, but not like this. Not Cam's tongue sliding in next to his finger while his hand held Noah so open he wanted to scream. Suddenly, the rub of the sheet against his dick was too much and he was close, God too close, but Cam backed off.

21

Cam crawled over him, dropping a kiss on his shoulder. The drawer of the nightstand creaked, and Cam clambered back on top of him, straddling one of his thighs. He nudged the inside of Noah's knee with his, pushing it toward his waist. Cam's finger was back inside before Noah had time to think, to process the sensation of cold lube and warm flesh against him.

"God, you do have a tight little ass." Cam's groan vibrated on Noah's spine.

His muscles shifted and relaxed as Cam's finger tickled nerves Noah never knew he had.

"That's it. Suck it right in," Cam murmured.

Noah was just relaxing into that rhythm when Cam slid in another finger. Slid wasn't quite it. Jammed was more like it. It fucking burned. Noah flinched, and then Cam's hand was on Noah's dick, pulling it down between his legs, and the burn eased into stinging, and then Noah was rocking back onto those fingers. Cam twisted them, and after a second of pain Noah felt a splash of pleasure from deep inside. He arched, tried to get back there, but Cam seemed to know all about it, and he did it again and again.

Every time he rubbed inside Noah, it felt better and better until Noah could hear himself moaning *yeah* with every thrust.

Cam's mouth grazed the small of Noah's back before forcing in another finger. If two had burned, three was fucking fire. Noah groaned, and Cam kissed his back and then his hip, sucking deep.

"Fucking hell, you're going to burn my dick off." Cam pulled his fingers free, and Noah buried his wince in the pillow.

He heard the tear of a condom wrapper. Seconds later slick latex was rubbing along the crack of his ass. Cam pulled on Noah's hips until he was up on his knees.

Noah wasn't completely naïve. He knew it was going to

hurt. There was no way it couldn't, at least not at first—unless maybe they took a week to get him ready. But they only had tonight, and Noah wasn't leaving until he'd had Cameron Lewis's dick up his ass. He could tell Cam it was his first time, and Cam might take it slow, murmur soft words and relax him, or Cam might change his mind completely and again, Noah wasn't leaving this room a virgin.

He thought he was ready for it, tried to breathe and relax and all that shit, but he quickly figured out that there's absolutely no way to be ready for a rock-hard dick forcing itself into your ass. He fought the urge to flinch away and held steady as Cam pushed in. He didn't stop, just kept coming and damn, Cam hadn't felt that big in his mouth, but now his dick felt like a goddamned traffic cone, and he kept going and how the fuck long was he, anyway?

"Fuck, fuck, *fuck*, Noah, you're gonna kill me. So tight."

Cam's balls finally hit Noah's ass, and Cam stayed there, panting. Noah's chest was heaving like he'd done a double lap under water. As Noah bit his lip against screaming *Get it out*, Cam moved his hands from Noah's hips, stroking his back and sides until Noah could feel how sweat-slicked his own skin was. Cam's hand wrapped around Noah's hips and tugged on his softened dick.

It didn't help much, his dick tried to rise, tried to find something to get excited about. But the memory of that oh-so-good rub of Cam's fingers inside had faded under this tearing, eye-watering stretch. Maybe the first time never got good, no matter what Noah had heard. Maybe he should tell Cam to move so he could get this over with.

Noah arched his back, and Cam slid deeper, groaning, "Yeah, baby, like that."

The endearment made Noah a little sick, like Cam couldn't

bother to remember his name anymore, that Noah had become a convenient hole to fuck.

Cam settled his hands back on Noah's hips, moving him forward and back as Cam fucked slow and deep. Noah twisted his hands in the sheet, feeling sweat break everywhere, his wrists, his knuckles, his scalp. He didn't know if he could do this, take it long enough to let Cam get off, and then Cam eased back all the way, stretching Noah right at the rim and when Cam sank back in, it didn't hurt anymore.

Every single nerve inside Noah lit up like a sparkler. His muscles opened and pulled Cam in deeper. Pleasure rolled through Noah in a sweet, hot blast that kept rushing around in his bloodstream. Fingers tightening on Noah's hips, Cam slammed deep, jerking him back to meet each thrust. So good, so good it was almost too much, good enough to scare Noah a little. How could he feel this good for this long? How was he ever going to let it stop?

Cam groaned as he arched into Noah, tight quick pants of *yeah, man* and *oh fuck*, falling into the rhythm of Cam's hips as they pistoned against Noah's ass.

Noah panted. "God, Cam, I didn't..." and it was harder to get the words out than he thought it could be. Every time Cam's dick speared him, speech flew out of Noah's head until he was reduced to spitting words out between each of Cam's powerful thrusts. "I...didn't...know...feel...like...this."

Cam's hips stuttered then stopped, his hands squeezing Noah's hips before kneading the muscles of his back. "Ah fuck, Noah, you should have told me."

"Why?" His ass throbbed around Cam's dick, and he just wanted him to move again. He rolled his hips.

"I wouldn't have, shit, I wouldn't have gone so hard." Cam's hands made a soothing pass down Noah's back again.

Noah pressed his lips together to keep back a groan of frustration. "You hear me complaining?"

Cam laughed again, and as much as that smug chuckle pissed Noah the hell off, he knew that it meant all that awkward shit was over, and Cam was going to keep fucking him.

"C'mon, Cam." Noah rocked as much as he could, but Cam was gripping his hips, keeping him still.

"You're a pushy bottom, aren't you?" Cam pressed his chest over Noah's back, mouthed the side of Noah's neck, the top of his shoulder. Noah rocked against him, trying to get that good friction again. Cam pressed his shins over Noah's calves and held him, driving into Noah with strokes so deep and so devastatingly slow that Noah swore he could feel every single vein, every ridge on Cam's dick, even through the rubber.

"If I'd have known, I'd've gone nice and slow like this." Cam dropped kisses on his neck and shoulders, his hips starting a swivel that forced sounds from Noah he never thought he could make. Noah's legs shook and couldn't hold him up anymore, and he fell forward under Cam's weight. Cam pinned Noah harder, a hand on his shoulder blade, legs forcing Noah's wide as Cam kept rolling his hips until Noah thought his whole nervous system was going to collapse on pleasure overload because he'd never felt anything like this.

Noah reached behind him, trying to get Cam closer, and Cam pulled Noah's hand away.

"Touch your cock, baby, make yourself come." Cam sped up his strokes until his balls were slapping against Noah's ass.

Noah gritted his teeth and dragged the words out. "Don't want to. Not yet." And he tightened his ass around Cam's dick.

"Oh fuck." Cam breathed, arching harder, faster. He leaned down again and laced his hands over Noah's. "Gonna have to beg for it then, babe."

Cam shifted higher against him, his cock driving into Noah from a different angle and that was it. The fucking gold medal thrust, because Cam was rubbing something that just pumped pleasure onto Noah's already overloaded nerves until he swore he could see spots behind his squeezed-shut lids, and he'd always thought that was some bullshit people made up to describe sex, but it was true. Purple, white, black, red sparks, his body shuddering as Cam slammed into Noah again and again, Cam's body keeping Noah pinned so that every stroke hit him and ripped another burst of that blinding pleasure from deep inside.

Noah knew the sounds he was making couldn't even be considered human anymore, and he didn't care if the whole hotel could hear him as long as Cam kept fucking him. The bed was rocking under the force of Cam riding him, shoving Noah right up to that edge where he had to come or die. He tried to pry his fingers loose.

"Wanna come now?"

Noah could only force out a strangled groan, but Cam released his hands, and Noah managed to get his right hand on his dick, to tug on the hard, hot skin. Cam pinned Noah flat with his hands on his shoulders again, but it didn't matter because it wasn't going to take much to push him over. He thumbed the head of his cock just as Cam slammed deep, and Noah's balls drew up, the last warning tingle shivering in his bones.

"Yeah, c'mon, baby."

Cam's mouth, hot and sucking hard on Noah's shoulder yanked the first blast from Noah's dick. Cam slammed another and another shot out of Noah, fucked him until his balls were dry, his dick soft and slick in his hand.

Noah felt Cam pull out, rough enough to make Noah wince,

and then Cam was straddling Noah's ass and from the sound of Cam's hand on his dick he'd stripped off the rubber.

"Hot fucking ass, baby. Squeezed me so hard."

Then Cam gasped, and Noah felt the first splash of warmth high up on his back, the next landing closer to the top of his ass. He wanted to count, see if he'd made Cam shoot as much as Noah had, but his brain was so fuzzy, and his legs were like blocks of cement. He couldn't even manage to roll out of the mess he'd made on the sheet, and he just didn't care. The last thing he remembered was Cam's mouth soothing the spot on his shoulder where he'd bitten him.

Dried come is never particularly pleasant, and Noah discovered that when you wake up smeared in it front and back, it really sucked. He peeled himself off the sheet. Of course, it sucked a lot worse when you woke up alone.

He looked around the room. Light streamed in from the space in the drapes, and the bright red numbers on the clock told him it was eight thirty-five. He tried to work up a little surprise and disappointment at finding the room silent and empty, but he couldn't. He'd pushed Cam into this, and Cam had never given Noah any kind of idea that he was getting anything from Cam but exactly what Noah had pushed for. If Noah had the crazy idea that they'd share a cup of coffee before going down to the brunch his parents were hosting for the out-of-town guests, that was his own problem.

Cam's luggage was gone, but he'd left the keycard on the desk and the do-not-disturb sign was gone from the door hook. Noah showered what was left of last night off his skin before he pulled his tuxedo pants and shirt back on and headed back to the room he was sharing with his cousin Bobby.

Bobby sat up when Noah stepped in the room. "Dude. Workin' that wedding hook-up. I covered for you with your mom."

"Thanks." Noah eyed the chair and the bed for a minute and then sat gingerly on the edge of the bed. He wasn't as sore as he expected to be, and that was kind of disappointing. Shouldn't there be something, something that might last a little longer than the already fading bruises on his hip and shoulder?

"So, who was it? The cousin from New York?"

"No one."

"Dude. Best kind." Bobby slapped him on the head as he disappeared into the bathroom.

Noah knew it was stupid, but he still kind of hoped Cameron would be there at the brunch, wanted some kind of confirmation that last night wasn't just one of his more elaborate wet dreams. He'd settle for a quick wink from one of those green-gold eyes.

His new sister-in-law came up to him while he was picking through the bacon, trying to find the most burned pieces. "A little too much celebrating?" she asked softly.

Noah forced a smile to his lips. "No. I'm fine." He was always fine. Everyone always talked about how happy he was, such a nice kid. "Uhm, have you seen Cameron this morning?" It was as casual as he could manage.

She shook her head. "Adam got a voice mail this morning, apologizing and saying he had to catch an early plane."

"Oh." He dug through the bacon with the tongs again. "Have a nice time in St. Thomas."

"It's the busy season for him, you know, Noah." Maria smiled and dropped a spoonful of eggs on his empty plate.

"Yeah."

She laid her hand on his shoulder and left him alone, leaving him to wonder if the girl his brother had just married didn't understand, or understood far too much.

Evidently Maria understood enough, because she passed on whatever news Cameron shared with Adam about his life. But the updates came less and less frequently, and by the time Noah was a senior in college, he didn't even know where Cam was living—in case he wanted to send him a Christmas card or something: "Hell of a fuck. Been having a nice life. Thanks for asking, you bastard." But that wasn't exactly fair.

It wasn't Cam's fault Noah had given Cam an unasked for starring role in Noah's life. But it would have been nice if Cam acknowledged him somehow, gave any kind of sign that Noah was more than Adam's brat kid brother. Noah knew that sex was just sex, but he'd known Cam all his life, damn it, and Noah had stupidly always expected Cam to be in it.

And a few years later he was, popping up on the recertification schedule, facing Noah over a podium. What really wasn't fair was that it didn't take more than the sight of Cam to make Noah's mouth go dry. That even after two serious relationships and more than a few good times, Noah could still feel every bit of him come to life at the sight of those sun-streaked curls and dark green eyes. Noah had had two months to think about how it was going to be when he saw Cam this time, and he wasn't about to blow it in the first hour. He pretended to concentrate on the handouts.

Chapter Two

Havers Safety instructors were drilled on the importance of uniform presentation, and Cameron had never been more grateful for the fact that he could do this recertification in his sleep. Because he might as well have been asleep for all the attention he was able to pay to the program with Noah Winthrop sitting in the front row. A whole new and improved Noah Winthrop. This Noah oozed a confidence that had almost knocked Cameron on his ass, and the muscle Noah had packed onto his tall frame had Cameron wondering every other minute how it would feel pressed against him.

He wouldn't say he hadn't thought about Noah since Adam's wedding, actually Cameron had kind of expected to hear something from Noah those first few months, and when Cameron didn't, he figured he hadn't screwed up too badly. When the haze of sex and champagne had worn off he'd wondered exactly what the protocol was for taking your best friend's *brother's* virginity.

Noah had looked years younger asleep than awake, with his arms wrapped around the pillow and those bangs over his face. As Cameron had watched Noah sleep that morning, a spurt of panic had folded his stomach in on itself. At the time, Cameron had barely known what it was, because he tended to avoid situations that would end in that kind of terrifying uncertainty. It wasn't his proudest moment, heading for the airport early to avoid facing Noah and Adam, but his gut seemed to think it was a pretty damned good plan, and his gut hadn't steered him wrong yet.

If Noah had given Cameron much thought after that night, Noah didn't show it now. Every time Cameron snuck a peek at Noah he was either watching the DVD or leafing through the handouts. It was ridiculous to even worry about it. It was a long time ago, and even if Cameron did know Noah better than any other guy he'd slept with it was just because they happened to grow up a block apart.

Cameron's dick decided that was pure bullshit by the time they got to the water part of the training. Noah stretching his arms before he dove into the pool made Cameron wish to hell they were doing this in wet suits. And Noah wet, Noah volunteering to be the spinal injury victim, the water beading on his nipples, sliding over his abs, his biceps, his pecs just made things worse. By the time the practice rescue was over, Cameron had decided that Noah had been put on this earth to torment Cameron for any past and future sins. He thanked God for the withering chill of the pool as he eased in to correct someone's technique.

He hadn't had this problem dealing with all the other incarnations of Noah he'd known. Unless you counted the time he'd let champagne and the flattering intensity of Noah's crush override sense and Cameron had fucked Noah's brains out, a memory which was not helping the cold water do its work. It was marginally easier when Noah wasn't the one stretched out on the spinal board, when he was only a participant and all Cameron had to worry about was the power Noah showed as he moved through the water, the way the rescue tube looked tiny in his hands, his effortless demonstration of the skills they were reviewing. Cameron spared a glance at the clock. He needed a

31

drink, and he needed to get laid. And with each tick of the clock salvation was getting closer.

When the final drill was complete, he called an end to the class. "CPR and First Aid starts at eight in the classroom tomorrow, final tests for recertification in the pool tomorrow afternoon."

Noah vaulted out of the pool in the deep end, one press of his arms sending him rocketing onto the deck, the weight of the water tugging his trunks down just far enough for Cameron to see the dip before that so-fuckable ass rounded. He shut his eyes and when he opened them, Noah'd disappeared into the locker room. And that was a good thing, Cameron reminded himself. Noah Winthrop was a complication Cameron's life did not need. As soon as the pool emptied, Cameron grabbed his bag and waved good-bye to the site coordinator.

Cameron stopped dead when he got into the parking lot. The brilliant Florida sun had vanished under dense clouds that promised rain in—if he could still read Gulf Coast weather patterns—about thirty minutes. He tossed his gear into the trunk of the rental car and slammed it, then glanced up to see if any of his students had exited in time to witness his mini temper tantrum.

He hadn't bothered to change out of his swim trunks and T-shirt—the possibility of running into a naked Noah in the locker room had the potential to be far more of a distraction than the eye candy Cameron had originally thought he was getting. If he was going to get that drink and the other necessities of not thinking about Noah underway, Cameron was going to have to go back to the hotel to change.

By the time he'd found a parking spot near the bar, the rain he'd known was coming hit and it hit sideways. Not that he'd expected anything less with the way his day was going.

This early in the afternoon the bar was almost empty. Two solo drinkers at the bar, one at a table. No one was going to get much use out of the rooftop tables, but there was a dance floor in the dimly lit downstairs. No DJ yet, but he was pretty sure there had been a jukebox down there last time he was here. Watching a couple of guys who'd been chased off the beach by the weather dance and make out was just what Cameron needed to get his mind off his confusing, fucked-up day. And maybe there was someone bored enough by the rain to entertain him for awhile.

He left the bartender a ten for his five-dollar Corona and made his way to the balcony overlooking the dance floor. There was one couple dancing.

Cameron wanted to curse out loud.

The taller guy was wrapped around his partner from behind, grinding to a song whose beat Cameron could barely hear over the rush of blood in his ears. *Noah* was wrapped around the smaller guy, a blue-striped shirt making him look even larger.

Cameron didn't know what was making his head pound like this until the guy reached up and cupped the back of Noah's head and the thought flashed through him. *I had that ass first. No matter what, that'll always be mine.* He caught the narrow neck of the bottle before it could slip through his fingers. He was jealous. Of some random guy with Noah? That was fucking ridiculous. Cameron didn't get jealous. He never had a reason to.

Certainly he wouldn't be jealous of the way Noah was grinding into that guy's ass because Cameron was a top. He always topped—except those two times when he should have known better. He should be looking at the other guy, and he definitely didn't wish he could switch places with him and feel what it was like to rest his head back against those shoulders.

Damn, the brat had gotten tall. Taller than his dad or Adam.

Cameron thought about abandoning his Corona and plans for the bar, but then Noah looked up and saw him, and while Cameron might prefer to avoid confrontations, he wasn't a pussy. He wasn't going to let Noah see that he'd chased Cameron off.

He took a seat at the end of the bar away from the other solo drinkers. The bartender came over immediately. Cameron waved him off since he'd barely started on the Corona, but he remedied that quickly enough, not even tasting the beer as it slid down his dry throat. The bartender had dropped off another in front of Cameron before Noah appeared and went up to the middle of the bar. His dance partner wasn't around.

"Where's your friend?" The question was out before Cameron thought about how it sounded. He glanced down at the half-empty second in his hand. Was it only his second?

Noah turned and flashed those damned dimples as he raked his hair back. "Last I saw him he had his tongue down his boyfriend's throat."

"Yeah? Because you guys looked pretty tight."

"His boyfriend doesn't dance, but he likes to watch him." Noah shrugged.

Cameron caught the bartender's eye and nodded at Noah. As Noah leaned in to place his order, his hips were almost up to the level of the bar. Cameron's brain decided to play a movie for him: Noah in nothing but that blue-striped shirt, ass tipped up over the bar, and damned if his brain wasn't even providing some kind of cheesy porn soundtrack. When he dragged his rational mind back on line, Noah was on the stool next to him.

"Thanks for the drink." Noah inclined the bottle in his

direction.

"Maybe I owed you one."

"Nah. Wasn't that big a deal." Only one dimple flashed with his half smile.

"Ouch." Cameron sucked on his lime wedge.

Noah's grin widened until it was creasing the corners of his cat-like eyes. "So."

"So. Still like the Yankees?"

"Even after the last eight seasons, yeah." Noah's gaze went down the length of him. "So. Still dress left, huh?"

Cameron spit out the lime and glanced at his lap. "Fucking hell, Noah, did you always watch me that closely?"

Noah was laughing. "Fishing for a compliment?"

Cameron could feel his cheeks burning, and he hardly ever blushed. He should have pussied out. Noah was going to drive him insane.

"Sorry, man. Maybe I owe *you* one."

"One what?" Cameron's mind rewound the video.

"A drink. Why?" There was that intense blue gaze again, the one that said Noah knew exactly what was playing on the screen in Cameron's brain. "What did you have in mind?"

If only it were that easy. Noah was even more gorgeous than he'd been as a teen, and there wasn't all that guilt about Adam's kid brother hanging over him anymore. But...why couldn't it be that easy?

"Are you living in Panama City now?"

"Actually I'm in Tallahassee, but I'm staying here for the training. I didn't feel like getting up at five to drive down."

"Where are you staying?"

"Why?" Noah had always been too fucking direct.

Cameron watched the rain still blurring past the bar's door. "Never mind."

Noah smiled again. "The Holiday Inn on 79. Room 314." He sucked on the neck of his beer.

Now the back of Cameron's neck was burning. He didn't remember everything about that night, but Noah's deep-throating skill coupled with his lung capacity had been something that Cameron didn't think he'd ever forget.

"Brat."

"Hmmm?" Somehow Noah managed to seem like he was looking up at him as he peered through his bangs. He had picked up some moves.

Cameron changed the subject. "Your folks still in Pensacola?"

"Yeah. Yours?"

Cameron nodded.

"Staying with them?" Noah asked.

"Havers is putting me up at the Majestic on the beach."

"Great weather for it." Noah's eyes were laughing at him again.

"Fuck you."

Noah just laughed and raised his eyebrows and then he put his mouth on the bottle again.

Cameron wondered what would happen if he reached out and yanked the bottle from Noah's hands, pulled him down and kissed him. Cameron didn't think Noah would mind. They'd go back to Noah's room and...and it would be twice as hard to get through the training tomorrow. Noah hardly needed any brownie points with the teacher with his skills, but Cameron took his job seriously. Even if it was only a retraining he needed to have his other head in control tomorrow.

"So how's Adam? Two boys, huh?"

Noah told him stories about his nephews, producing pictures from his wallet. They talked through another round, and Cameron hadn't noticed that the bar had filled up until someone leaned against him to order a drink.

Noah looked down at his watch. "I'm gonna grab some dinner and head back to the hotel."

There it was. Noah was a grown man, gorgeous, and still interested. The last time he'd tucked his wallet in his pocket, Cameron could see Noah was half hard, and he doubted it was a discussion of the Yankees' pitching staff that had done it. Cameron would be gone the day after tomorrow; Noah knew it. They could be adults about it all.

"We could split something on Havers food allowance." He watched Noah straighten from the stool and got up because then Noah was just too damned tall.

Noah looked at him, and for once Cameron couldn't figure out what was going on behind those bright eyes.

"You know what? I think I'm just going to go back to my hotel. See you tomorrow, Cam. Thanks for the drink." Noah clapped him on the shoulder, like Cameron was the one four years younger, and left the bar.

Cameron tapped his fingers against the steering wheel in time with the rain as he sat in the Holiday Inn parking lot at quarter after ten. The same nagging tension that had been chewing on his stomach since Buffalo was back and now he couldn't blame it on cold weather. Noah had turned him down. Cameron couldn't believe how much that bugged him. It wasn't an unequivocal slam, but Noah hadn't surprised Cameron like that since the brat had crawled on top of Cameron ten years ago. If Cameron had ever known a sure thing, it was that Noah would be back in Cameron's bed if he so much as crooked a finger.

He didn't mind a little chase, but he never bothered if he wasn't completely sure at the outset that the guy wanted to be caught. The fact that his sure thing had blown up in his face was something he just couldn't accept.

He pushed open the car door. Maybe he'd regret this, but he'd regret going back to his own hotel with that empty feeling in his stomach more.

Room 314 opened to his first knock. Noah was still in faded jean shorts and his blue-striped shirt, though the button on his fly was undone and his shirt was hanging open. Cameron was a little afraid his mouth was hanging open, too. If he hadn't already seen what six years had done for Noah's body at the pool, he'd be standing there gaping until Noah laughed at him again.

Noah rested his hand on the top of the door and held it open after Cameron had stepped in. Noah's eyes were still unreadable.

Cameron started to speak but rejected everything that came to mind. At last, he looked up and saw that Noah's knuckles were white where they gripped the door, and Cameron didn't need to say anything at all.

He reached for Noah with a hand on his neck and one on his ass, and Noah fell against Cameron with a groan, the door slamming shut as Noah kicked it.

"Son of a bitch, Noah, why'd you do that?" He licked his neck.

"I didn't really want you to take me out to dinner and you

hadn't offered anything else." Noah's hand slipped into his curls and he kissed him.

"Bullshit," Cameron said when he came up for air.

"Oh, so you said, 'I want to have sex with you, Noah?' I must have missed that."

"Are we gonna talk or fuck?"

"You started it."

"I did this time." Cameron pulled Noah's head down with one hand and cupped his ass to get him closer.

Noah's tongue was as energetic as he remembered it, devouring his mouth like it was his last meal. Cameron held his chin to slow him, easing him until they were just tasting each other's lips with teeth and tongues.

Cameron lifted his arms as Noah's hand slid under his T-shirt, let him tug it over his head and fling it away. Noah's thumbs brushed Cameron's nipples as his hands stroked his ribs. Cameron licked under Noah's ear, before leaning back to watch those big hands spread across Cameron's ribs, a shade lighter than his skin. Then Noah's long fingers were tugging and twisting on Cameron's nipples with the right amount of pressure to send a pulse to his balls. His head dropped back and Noah's tongue and lips were on Cameron's throat, his collarbone, hands moving lower. If he remembered right, this was where things had gotten out of control last time.

He shoved Noah's shirt off his shoulders and while Noah struggled with the cuffs, Cameron stepped back and started to peel off his jeans.

The sight of Noah trying to wiggle free of his shirt made Cameron smile. "Need some help with that?"

Noah finally freed an arm. "Got it, thanks."

"Need help with the rest?"

"No, thanks."

"'Cause I can't wait to see that tight ass of yours again."

Noah's shorts hit the floor, and he reached out and rubbed a hand over Cameron's ass. "Who said you were the one getting a piece of ass tonight?"

Cameron almost tripped on the pile of denim at his feet. "I—Noah, I don't—"

"Oh my God, Cam, you should see your face."

"What? You can't just—" Because he couldn't have been thinking about Noah fucking him when he watched Noah dance. Would never want to be the one Noah ground into from behind.

"Assume and make an ass out of you and me?"

If Cameron wasn't already naked, he'd be at the door. What had happened to the guy who'd do anything to get Cameron to wink at him? When the fuck did this get so complicated?

"Relax, Cam."

God, Noah's hands were huge, covering Cameron's shoulders.

"You can try to improve on your performance," Noah said as his hands and mouth started to trail down the center of Cameron's chest.

"Improve—"

"Provided you still give good rim jobs and brought your own lube and condom."

"Ahh...in my jeans." Improve his performance. The little shit.

Noah's mouth was just above his navel.

"If I remember this correctly, I'd better be sitting down." Cameron's legs already felt the strain of holding him up as his body remembered the way Noah had taken him deep.

Noah steered Cameron toward the bed until he was sitting on the edge, legs sprawled in front of him.

"So my performance doesn't need improving on?" Noah's eyes flashed.

"Shut up and suck me, Noah."

Noah was still grinning when he knelt between his legs and licked the head, sending that first jolt of pleasure into Cameron's body. Noah slicked Cameron's dick, wet lips soft down one side and up the other. He mouthed his way down again, and then took Cameron's sac in his mouth, tongue rolling under his balls, while Noah rubbed beneath with his fingers. Cameron's legs started to shake, and he gave up keeping the gasps from slipping past his clenched teeth.

Holy shit, Noah hadn't even sucked him yet and already the skin of Cameron's dick was so tight it vibrated. Cameron stroked his hand through those long silky bangs, trying to urge Noah back up, but right where he was felt so damned good. Cameron bit back the words before they could spill out. One thing the grown-up Noah didn't need was any more confidence. Cocky son of a bitch.

Damned perfect cocksucking son of a bitch.

Noah's hand went to work on Cameron's dick, like he wasn't already primed enough for his mouth, his throat. Did he want him to fucking beg, was that it? "Noah."

Thank God, that was enough. Noah wrapped his lips around the crown, tongue lapping the weeping slit while his lips played with the underside and then he was sliding down slowly, tight and wet and his tongue... Cameron's hand yanked at Noah's hair as his lips sealed around the base, meeting the ring of his fingers around the root. He swallowed once and sucked back off just as slowly. When his teeth grazed the head exactly right, Cameron shuddered and clamped down all his muscles because his balls were taking that hike up, and no way was he going to shoot like this was his first fucking blowjob even if Noah could apparently suck a baseball through a straw.

Noah went deep again, the velvet of his throat milking, pulsing around the head of Cameron's dick, and his gasp was so loud it echoed in the room despite the background chatter of the TV. He glanced down to find those sexy, tilted blue eyes watching him as Noah's cheeks hollowed around his cock when he sucked back up. Cameron shut his eyes and bucked toward Noah's mouth.

Noah's tongue swirled around the crown at the top of every stroke, flicking the knot of nerves under the head, tracing the vein as he went back down. It was slow and torturous but damned close to getting Cameron off, and he wasn't ready for that to happen yet. He tugged on Noah's hair and dragged him off. The sound when Noah's lips finally pulled off was so perfectly obscene Cameron had to tug his own balls down.

Noah looked up at him, a question in his eyes, his hand stroking lightly up and down Cameron's spit-wet cock. "No rented pants this time."

Cameron dragged Noah onto the bed. "No. But we're switching."

Noah leaned up on his elbow, his hand dragging down over Cameron's hip. "Really?"

"Not like that." Cameron rasped their stubbled jaws against each other and whispered in Noah's ear. "I'm going to suck you until you come and then I'm going to eat you open and then I'm going to fuck you into orbit. And this time you're going to tell me if I go too fast. Got it?"

Noah's hand tightened on Cameron's hip. He liked it when intentions were clear, it made for smooth sailing, and his partners always seemed to appreciate the direct approach. From the hitch in Noah's breathing, he was no exception. He nodded, scraping their cheeks together.

"Good."

Cameron pressed Noah onto his back and tugged his hips down to the edge of the bed. He braced his hands inside Noah's knees and started at the edge of his tan line, teasing the insides of his thighs with mouth and tongue before following up with a stroke of thumbs. Noah leaned up on his elbow to watch, and when Cameron winked he saw the flush start to spread from Noah's cheeks into his neck. By the time Cameron was teasing the top of Noah's hipbone, the flush had spread into his chest, visible even under his tan.

Cameron took a deep breath, inhaling Noah's sweat and musk and the underlying scent of chlorine that never seemed to get out of your skin when you worked around pools. The smell just made Cameron want to taste, and he wrapped his lips around the shiny red head bobbing in front of him. Noah's hips bucked, and Cameron pushed Noah's thighs down, slicking Noah's dick with his spit. Cameron had never quite managed to deep throat, and even if he could he'd never manage it with Noah.

The dick brushing his lips was at least as long as his own and thickening as he watched. But Cameron was really good at coordinating his hands and mouth. Noah seemed to think so too, because as soon as Cameron lapped his tongue around the head in time with the quick jerk of his hand, Noah collapsed back against the bed.

Cameron curled his tongue around that slippery, salty weight in his mouth, tightened his lips and began to bob to meet his twisting hand. He glanced up to see Noah struggle up on his elbows again, but after a few hard sucks, he'd fallen back

43

with a groan that sounded like Cameron's name. He let Noah thrust a little, the knowledge that Cameron was driving Noah to the edge, that those groans, that flush was for him, made Cameron's own cock jerk.

Noah's scent got stronger, the taste of precome filling Cameron's mouth as he sucked it from the slit. His tongue made a lightning-quick figure eight around the head that dragged a gut-teasing whimper from Noah, and Cameron sucked hard, lips pressed under the head.

"Cam." The groan slid back up into that whimper. "Gonna...gonna..."

Cameron pulled off for a second. "Yeah, you are."

And he rubbed the head against his lips before he sucked Noah back in, pressing against the satiny skin beneath his balls until he arched up into the roof of Cameron's mouth, flooding him through spasm after spasm until Cameron couldn't swallow fast enough. He wiped his mouth on the edge of the sheet and watched Noah fight to get his breathing under control. The flush was slowly fading from his chest.

"God, Cam, hope you're happy. I'm dead."

"We'll see. You're young yet."

Noah managed to get an elbow underneath him. "And you're ancient?"

Thirty had stung. More than Cameron thought it would. And fuck if his thirtieth wasn't the first time he'd gotten this damned hollow feeling. It had started bugging him again last week in Buffalo, the same steady thrum of emptiness that had dragged him out to Noah's room at the Holiday Inn tonight.

Noah wouldn't be twenty-six for another month. Cameron remembered Noah's birthday, April fifteenth, tax day, the same as Cameron's mom. Yeah, thirty didn't bounce back like twenty-five.

"Roll," Cameron said.

"Huh?"

"I believe you requested a rim job before you'd let me fuck you."

"Oh."

But Cameron still had to flip him, and Noah was quite a load to shift, even with muscles gone limp from his orgasm. "You could help a little."

"You sucked my brains out, Cam."

This was the Noah he remembered, pliant and breathless from Cameron's attention. It didn't feel as oppressive as it had years before, just made Cameron want to get Noah there again, to know that no matter how cocky he'd become, he was still the Noah whose eyes had followed Cameron from under the brim of that too big Yankees hat. His gut got a bit less hollow.

"Yeah, and now I'm going to make you forget you ever had 'em."

Noah twisted and finally Cameron managed to get the uncooperative brat on his stomach, legs sprawled off the bed, his ass in the air. Cameron grabbed a pillow and shoved it under Noah's hips to tip him higher.

He fished the little lube packet and condom from his jeans and tossed them on the bed. Placing his hands on Noah's back, he felt the muscles jump and twitch. He stroked hard down over Noah's ass to his thighs and back up, pressing enough to watch the blood rush to the skin, sensitizing it. Noah's toes dug into the carpet next to Cameron's knees. He pulled on the skin of Noah's ass, stretching it until he moaned and arched off the pillow.

"Hold still."

"Make—"

So Cameron did. He pinned Noah open, got a deep breath of chlorine-scented musk and swept him with his tongue. Noah froze.

"All right?"

"Yeah," Noah's answer was pitched an octave above his usual voice. "Just don't want you to stop."

Cameron smiled as he laid another stripe with his tongue from balls all the way up. Noah's tense muscles shivered under Cameron's hands.

"You can move, babe. I won't stop." Cameron flicked his tongue over the soft skin covering hard muscle, pulled the crease wider with his thumbs.

Noah tried to squirm closer, and Cameron teased him some more, a quick flick and another long lick.

"God." Noah panted, and Cameron leaned back to watch the shudder ripple along Noah's dark-furred thighs.

Cameron couldn't resist running his hands up Noah's legs again, thumbs diving into the crease and stretching him. Noah's foot lifted for an instant, rubbing Cameron's thigh as it came back down, and Cameron had the impression that it had turned from a kick to a caress at the last minute. He smiled. He was done teasing anyway.

The sound Noah made when he speared him with his tongue sent Cameron from hard and twitching to gotta fuck or die. He groaned against Noah's skin, and that just made Noah moan louder. Cameron licked the muscle soft and open until he could slide both thumbs in next to his tongue, the shivering heat against his fingers driving every last bit of blood from his head until he had to stop and rest his forehead against Noah's ass.

"God, Cam, get in me. Now."

That was the smartest thing Noah'd ever said. Cameron shoved him up onto the bed, scrambling for the lube and the condom.

Noah was twisted in the middle of the mattress, and Cameron felt his own cock leak when he saw how thick Noah's dick was. Noah stroked himself slowly. The sight of that sweet dark crown breaking through his tanned fingers made Cameron swallow hard, tasting Noah on his tongue.

"Gotta fuck you, babe. C'mon."

"M'ready."

"Get on your knees."

Noah stared hard for a long minute, hand still stroking his dick, but if he had something to say, he changed his mind and rolled onto his stomach.

"You're going to tell me if you need me to slow down this time, right?"

"Not gonna need to."

Cameron took Noah at his word and slicked two fingers before sliding them in. Noah tightened and relaxed against him. The smooth clench of those muscles on his fingers had Cameron's dick leaking and jerking, and he swore he wasn't going to rush it this time, but he was already curling his fingers, pressing down until Noah's pants turned into a long moan.

"Now."

"You're still a pushy bottom."

But Cameron suited up in record time, pouring more lube over the latex, almost afraid to smooth it down before he wasted the rubber on his own damn hand. He gripped the base hard and rubbed the tip around, gliding over the ring of muscle until Noah was trying to push back onto him. Cameron pressed in slowly, but Noah arched and slammed back against him.

"Holy fucking hell, Noah." Cameron had to tighten his fingers like a cock ring. Noah's muscles squeezed him so fucking close to orgasm he couldn't see for a minute. He was pretty sure the near whiteout was because there wasn't a drop of blood left anywhere in his body but in his aching cock.

Noah tried to start rocking, and Cameron considered grabbing Noah's hips and pounding away, but since he was supposed to be improving on last time, that wouldn't be much of a showing. He settled back on his calves, bringing Noah with him.

That earned Cameron another sexy whimper as rocking and squirming, Noah opened his legs over Cameron's thighs. Now that Cameron had managed to get control of himself he was going to take his time. The bathroom and dresser mirrors reflected each other, giving him a double view of Noah's face and chest. Cameron watched his own hands slide from Noah's hips over his flushed chest. He brought his hand back down, following the dark hair from Noah's navel, pressing hard just above his cock, down against the bone until Noah clenched around him again.

"Fuck, move, please, Cam, please."

"You do it. Fuck yourself." He lifted Noah's hips and pulled him back.

"Shit," Noah breathed, rocking into a rhythm that milked Cameron's dick with slick, tight muscles and a burning heat he could feel even through the latex. Cameron kissed across the wide shoulders in front of him while Noah worked himself on Cameron's cock, coming down to meet every upward thrust of his hips.

"That's it." Cameron swept his hands up again, thumbs rubbing hard against Noah's nipples.

Noah shuddered, and his head slumped forward onto his chest. Cameron couldn't take his eyes off the sight of Noah in the mirror, his hair falling over his face, his chest arching and curling as he impaled himself again and again on Cameron's dick. Cameron licked the sweat from Noah's neck and shoulders, cursing Noah's height and wishing he were tall enough to reach his lips.

"God, Cam, God, please, I can't, I need…"

But Cameron wanted to watch it, wanted to see the moment Noah lost control, see the pleasure break across his face.

"Can you come like this?" Cameron let his hands rest on Noah's hips, pulling him faster, fucking up deeper.

"Don't know."

"Try." Cameron grabbed Noah's fist where it ground against his thigh and brought it to his cock, used Noah's own thumb to smear the precome over the head and down the hard satin shaft.

Noah shook again, his inner muscles quivering around Cameron's dick. Cameron kept his eyes on the mirror as he sank his teeth into Noah's shoulder blade and watched those wide lips part in a groan. Noah's hand was halting as he stroked his dick, slower than the rhythm of the reflections moving together.

"Fuck, Noah, you should see yourself."

Noah's head came up, and Cameron watched him meet his own gaze head on, felt and watched the shudder echo through them both as Noah realized what Cameron was seeing. Noah's hand worked faster on his dick.

"Look so fucking sexy like this, babe. So fucking hot with my dick in your ass."

Noah's eyes squeezed shut, his hand moving faster and faster as Cameron's hips jerked into him.

"Watch us. C'mon, Noah. Watch yourself come."

Noah groaned and his hand stuttered. "Harder, please." But his eyes opened again.

Cameron dug his fingers into Noah's hips and drove up as hard as he could, slamming Noah back down onto him. Noah's fingers glistened with precome as he fucked into his own fist. Deeper, sharper sounds broke from his bitten lips. Then his brow furrowed as his cheeks and jaw relaxed, his head dropped back onto Cameron's shoulder, and the first shot landed on the footboard. Cameron flexed his hips up into Noah as his hand twisted and pulled rope after rope out of his dick until his body collapsed.

With an arm around Noah's chest, Cameron eased Noah back onto his knees as gently as he could, the fire in Cameron's balls close to boiling out his dick from the way Noah's muscles had turned to a vise around Cameron's dick when Noah came. *So close, oh fuck, so close.*

Cameron stretched Noah's hands out to grab the footboard. "Hold on."

Noah was still making those sounds when a dozen quick, short strokes took Cameron right over the edge, pulse roaring in his ears as the lightning shot through him, jerked him so hard the aftershocks felt like coming all over again. Just in time he softened his mouth on Noah's shoulder before leaving a bruise that would be visible in class tomorrow.

Cameron tasted the salt on Noah's neck, took another deep breath of sweat and come and chlorine and eased out to flop onto his back. Tying off the condom, Cameron took feeble aim at the wastebasket. The resulting splat suggested he'd hit the wall instead. Noah was stretched out beside him, head turned to face him. Cameron lifted the sweaty strands of hair off Noah's neck and stroked down his back.

"So? Any improvement?"

Noah sighed and arched his brows. "Points for effort."

"Brat." Cameron slapped Noah's ass, rolled off the bed and headed for the bathroom.

Noah stretched out along the sheets, enjoying the fact that the wet spot was somewhere around his feet. It didn't matter anyway because when he had the energy, they could just move to the other bed. He listened to the water running in the bathroom and smiled into the pillow.

He might not have been able to hold out long, but at least he'd gotten Cam to come to him. Any hope of staying aloof had evaporated as soon as Cam touched him. Somehow just a look, just the curve of Cam's mouth, could make Noah forget he was the aquatics director at Tallahassee Community College, had been the captain of the Division III champion water polo team. Just that smile could make everything disappear in a rush of heat and want that made him feel fifteen again—without the annoying teenage confusion and angst.

"Here." Cam tossed him a towel and a wet washcloth and picked up his jeans.

The giddy feeling turned to nausea. He didn't know if he were more disgusted with himself or Cam.

He watched Cam tug the jeans up over his hips. "At least you didn't wait till I was asleep this time."

Cam had the balls to stare like he had no idea why Noah was pissed.

"Try not to trip as you run out the door."

"What the fuck, Noah?"

"Exactly. You know, I thought maybe we could do that again. Watch a movie. Talk."

"I've got a class to teach tomorrow."

"And I've got a class to take and tests to pass. So we'll sleep."

Cam smoothed down his T-shirt and leveled a stare at Noah that chased the nausea away with a desire that was no less frustrating. "No. We won't."

"And would that be so bad?"

Cam shrugged. "See you tomorrow."

At least he picked the condom off the floor and threw it out, not that Noah watched him leave or anything.

He should've just let Cam go with a careless "See you tomorrow" or maybe he should have faked a snore and not said a word. Noah was fucking hopeless. He didn't know why he'd thought tonight would be any different from the last time. No matter what he'd told himself, he'd known exactly how tonight was going to go.

Most of the guys he'd dated expected him to top. There was Kevin, four months of insisting on half and half—and being oddly OCD about keeping track of it. Then Joey, who'd lasted one month past their year anniversary, who'd liked Noah to top exclusively. Despite all that experience, Noah had known that the second Cam touched his dick Noah would roll over and beg for it like a bitch.

After all, wasn't that why he'd spent the past week stretching himself? He'd been so damned sure he'd finally get Cam to want him like he'd wanted Cam all those years. Noah was an idiot.

He sat up and punched the headboard. Now he was an idiot with sore knuckles. An idiot who still wanted Cameron

Lewis more than he'd ever wanted anything in his fucking life.

Chapter Three

Noah had planned out perfectly how he was going to act when he saw Cam again, but Noah hadn't planned on how he was going to act the day after a night that played out the same way as the one six years ago. Even if it was a night when the sex was mind-blowingly better than he remembered.

So he didn't rush to get to the training early, and still ended up in the front row. Cameron was wearing glasses. The gold earpieces disappeared almost unnoticed into his curls and the rimless lenses magnified the green of his eyes. How did he look so fucking sexy at seven forty-five in the morning? Noah felt like he'd been dragged through a hedge backward—and was sure he looked like it, too.

Cam didn't smile when he saw him, just glanced up for a minute and then went back to leafing through the binder on the podium. There were almost always minute changes to the CPR course every year—at least the way Havers Safety wanted it administered. Noah focused his attention because there was sure to be some small detail on the test designed to trip people up. The morning went faster than he'd thought it would. When he and Cam finally met over a resuscitation dummy, Noah said, "I didn't know you wore glasses."

"Couldn't get my contacts in this morning." Cam's tone suggested that it was somehow Noah's fault. "Head's not back far enough." Cam looked down at the dummy, and Noah repositioned the head.

Even with the variations from year to year, Noah could do this, was good at this. But with Cam's implacable stare fixed on him, his confidence swirled and drained away as if someone had pulled a plug out from underneath him. Instructor trainers never usually said anything, unless you were doing something wrong, just gave you updates on the "victim's" condition. But Noah's breathing and counting sounded more awkward and loud than they ever had in the seven years he'd been doing this, ringing in the silence before Cam moved on to check out the next student.

Noah could hear Cam's voice get warmer and more encouraging as he worked with the next pair.

The guy Noah had been sharing the dummy with breathed an exaggerated sigh of relief. "Jeez, what you do to piss him off? I've never seen anyone with Havers act like that."

Since Noah doubted "Let him fuck me" was really an appropriate response, he shrugged.

The written test was the last thing before the lunch break, and Noah was the first one done. He went up and put the paper on the table at the front of the room, and Cam never even looked up. Fuck that. Cam didn't get to act like nothing had happened again. And he sure as hell didn't get to act like he didn't even know who Noah was.

Noah ate a sandwich in his truck, watching to see if Cam left the building before the pool session. When he hadn't come out by twenty after twelve, Noah went back inside and changed into his trunks. Cam disappeared behind a door just as Noah got onto the pool deck. Noah glanced down at his bruised knuckles and decided not to punch the tiles. The deck was dry, perfect for stalking over and yanking open the door.

Cam turned around in surprise, two test tubes in his hands. The pumps swished and thumped alongside them. Once again, Noah had made an absolute ass of himself. Cam hadn't come in here to avoid him, he was only testing the water.

Noah leaned against the door. "Since when do you work for the college?"

"I told the kid to go get some lunch. I can guard till he gets back for the class." Cam held the tubes up to the light and marked the readings on the clipboard. He dumped out the test tubes and closed up the kit before turning back to Noah. The light reflected off his glasses, making it harder than ever to read his expression.

Noah shoved his bangs back from his forehead.

"What happened to your knuckles?"

Ah shit. Noah stared down at the dark bruises. He'd been able to hide them during CPR since he'd been wearing gloves. "Bar fight." He raised his eyes and grinned.

Cam's brow furrowed, and for a second Noah thought Cam was actually going to believe that story.

"I wasn't sleepy after all," he added.

Cam's lips parted as he started to smile. God, he was even sexier in those glasses. This was Noah's Cam, the Cam he was when they were alone. The Cam who looked at Noah like Cam wanted him for breakfast, lunch and supper.

Noah held up his bruised hand. "Want to kiss it and make it better?"

"Asshole. No rewards for being self-abusive." Cam caught Noah's arm as he pushed it forward. Cam's thumb brushed across the inside of Noah's wrist, the pressure on his pulse making his blood pump faster. "Maybe later."

"What's wrong with now?"

Cam twisted their wrists to look at his dive watch. "Class starts in twenty-five minutes."

Noah freed his arm and grabbed Cam's hips to pull him tight. "And you think it's going to take that long? That's cute, Cam."

With a tight grip on Noah's shoulders, Cam shoved Noah into the door. Their breath brushed each other's lips as Noah shifted his grip on Cam's hips until the swell of Cam's dick pressed against his own.

"I can get you off in ten with my mouth." He murmured the promise right into Cam's mouth before dropping to his knees, taking Cam's trunks with him.

Noah's stomach jumped with satisfaction when he saw that Cam was already half hard. He gripped the base of Cam's dick and slid the tip across his lips. He heard a beep above him and looked up to see Cam setting his watch.

"Nine minutes fifty-five seconds."

"Competitive much?"

Cam braced his hands against the door and spread his legs, swirling his hips so that his cock rubbed all over Noah's face. Noah sat back on his heels. Cam glanced down. "Nine thirty-five."

"What do I get if I win?" Noah dug his hands into Cam's hips to keep him steady for a teasing lick from his tongue.

"Uh—you get laid tonight."

"I think I'm getting laid anyway." He wet the head with his lips again. Cam jerked toward him, but Noah held his hips. "Sex and breakfast."

"You want...me to buy you breakfast?" Cam was straining toward him. Noah mouthed the side of Cam's dick.

"Close enough." Noah took Cam into his mouth.

"Eight—ahhhh fuck—twenty."

Noah eased down, molding his lips over his teeth. Cam fit perfectly in his mouth, just enough of a stretch to make Noah relax his jaw, soften his lips. His tongue sought the ridges and veins as he took Cam deeper, swallowed, gulped Cam's cock into his throat. The thump of the water through the pumps hid the sound of Cam's breaths, masked his moans but Noah could feel the muscles jumping under his hands.

He eased back, sucking hard on the ridge and flicking the slit with his tongue, salty drops springing up behind every stroke. He loved this. The power of holding someone in your mouth, his heat and weight rolling across your tongue while you drove him out of his mind. And knowing that he was holding Cam this way was enough to make Noah's own dick leak into the mesh of his swim trunks.

He pulled off enough to push words past his lips onto the smooth red flesh. "Fuck my mouth." He let one of his hands trail down from Cam's hips, slid fingers between the cheeks of Cam's ass, skimmed the sensitive ring before rubbing hard against the tight silky skin of his perineum.

"Uhn."

It might have been a thunk from the pumps, but since Cam's hips started pumping him forward between Noah's lips, he decided it was from Cam. Cam's hand wrapped around the back of Noah's head and offered him a layer of protection from the door as Cam drove against the back of Noah's throat.

Noah wished he could twist his neck enough to watch Cam's face, tried to picture what this was doing to him, but all Noah could do was hold on as Cam lost control. Rough affection flooded him as he let Cam use the heat and slick of his mouth against his dick, let Cam slam against his lips until they felt like they'd split, sensation pounding in him until Noah's own need felt like a black hole in his stomach, his dick forced up against the elastic edge of his trunks.

And he wanted it. Wanted to hang here balanced on the wave of pleasure and pain, knowing Cam was riding the same crest, holding it as long as he could before he was gone, bursting in Noah's mouth, salt, smoke, a burn like a shot of tequila in his throat. Noah drank him down, his tongue flicking the tip as the last shudders drained him, and then only Noah's arm around his waist was holding him up.

A beeping echoed over the swoosh of the pumps and pounding in Noah's temples.

Cam managed a chuckle. "You can have fucking filet mignon for breakfast. Goddamn." His thumb rubbed over Noah's swollen lip, painting it with the come spilling from the corners of his mouth.

Noah sucked on it for a minute, Cam's hand playing through his hair.

"I should have pulled out. If I'd split your lip..."

Acid burned through the thick come in Noah's throat. "Are you—?"

"No, shit, of course not. I would have told you. I get tested at least once a year." Cam took a deep breath. "You know, even if I spring wood every time I smell chlorine now, that was worth it. You've got a hell of a mouth on you, babe."

"That kind of reaction to chlorine could be a bit awkward in our line of work."

"Just a bit." Cam pulled Noah to his feet with a grip on his forearm, and since Noah felt like his dick was sticking out about an extra eight inches from his body he wasn't surprised when it brushed Cam's stomach. "Shit." Cam looked at his watch.

"Yeah. I'll be all right." *In an hour or two. If I have an ice bucket. And maybe castrate myself.* Noah moved away from the door. "Just gimme a minute."

"Check the flow meter."

"Huh?" Noah stepped toward the pump.

Cam came up behind him. "I think we need to check the flow meter." Cam put his hands around Noah's waist and loosened the tie on his trunks.

"Uh—" There had to be people out in the pool area by now. The facility's lifeguard could be coming in here to check...anything. And the kid would find Cam's hand on Noah's dick, his own hand on his dick as Cam reached up and put Noah's hand over the burning skin. His own hand was cool, Cam's hot as their fingers wove together.

"Show me. Show me how you like it. I want to feel it."

Oh God, Noah was so hard, and the chance of discovery didn't seem to be doing a thing to change his dick's mind about how good that pressure felt. In fact, the thought that someone might see them like this, that Cam would risk this, made Noah's balls hike up close to his body. He started tugging, Cam mirroring the strokes, his lips grazing the back of Noah's neck.

"Almost," Noah panted. "Harder."

Cam's fingers tightened between Noah's, the dry, rough rub just on the sweet side of pain.

"Come for me, Noah. Made me feel so good, babe."

That was *it*. Noah's body didn't care about anything but grabbing that release. He rocked into the pull of their hands, feeling the swell start at the base of his spine until it burned through him and he collapsed into warm, deep spasms of pleasure, knowing Cam was there to catch him as his legs gave out.

Cameron bent his knees as Noah sagged into him, head sliding down on Cameron's shoulder. He wrapped his arms around Noah's waist, feeling an inexplicable need to mouth his way along Noah's neck to his jaw, to tip his mouth back and kiss him—just to kiss him. Because he could.

Voices sounded outside the door, the sounds echoing off the tiles, and Cameron shook off the urge. He led Noah's hand to one of the pipes and eased his weight onto his feet. Crossing to the eye-wash station, he rinsed his hands and dried them on a towel.

"Here." He tossed back the damp towel. "You can...uh...turn up the acid. If you need a minute. It's an interesting new flow meter, isn't it?"

"Jesus, Cam. Anybody might have walked in."

"Not really."

Cameron picked up a lanyard the young guard had handed him and jangled the keys at the end.

Noah's eyes narrowed. "Then how did I get in?"

"Oh shit." Cameron felt lightheaded in a way that had nothing to do with his dick. If that door was unlocked—holy fucking God, he could have thrown away his career. What the hell was he thinking?

Actually he wasn't. At least, not with the right head. And he never seemed to when Noah was around. The sooner Cameron got on that plane to Indiana tomorrow the better off he'd be. And for the rest of the afternoon, he'd have to keep his distance from that floppy-haired, blue-eyed piece of sin on legs.

Alphabetical order placed Noah second to last as they ran through the practical part of the test. Noah'd breezed through the time trials. Now there was only the last rescue.

When Noah had the victim safe on the deck in record time, gloves snapped onto wet hands, he began CPR after listening to Cameron's report on the dummy's vitals. It was all perfectly routine, no different from any of the hundreds of recertifications he'd be doing this spring. And then Noah started chest compressions. Water poured off Noah's shoulders as his weight sank his hands down into the sternum of the dummy.

Cameron couldn't tear his eyes away from the rhythmic press of Noah's shoulders, his forearms, every muscle delineated with strength. Cameron had never noticed how fucking sexual CPR was, the rise and fall of Noah's chest with the thrusts. How the hell was Cameron ever going to get this image out of his mind? First the pump room and now this.

He felt eyes on him and realized Noah had completed more than three minutes of CPR and would have to keep going until Cameron told him to stop.

Cameron swallowed. "End with this cycle."

Noah hung around and played water victim while Leo Zanewski finished his test. Leo was handsome and ripped, but watching him do CPR on the dummy didn't quite have the same effect—at least Cameron could be grateful for that. Maybe he should tell Noah he'd changed his mind about tonight. Cameron snuck a glance at Noah while Leo was doing chest compressions.

Despite the fact that Noah's mouth had sucked Cameron dry an hour ago, he felt a kick of want echo deep and low at the sight of him leaning against the lifeguard stand, arms folded, ankles crossed. One more time wouldn't hurt. Cameron was still leaving tomorrow; this month was an endless series of recertifications all over the map. Noah caught Cameron looking and returned his stare. All the intensity and energy of those blue eyes burning for him, and no matter how much Cameron's brain might try to warn him that it was a bad plan, he was going to have Noah again—and again if there was time. And then—well, it was just sex. Good sex. Holy-fucking-God good sex.

And Noah'd grown into a great guy. Maybe Cameron would try to see him if he ended up in North Florida again. And if he didn't, Cameron would still leave things much better than he did when he'd freaked out after Adam's wedding, which was a bonus. You didn't often get a chance to fix things you'd screwed up. Cameron flashed a wink at Noah and told Leo Zanewski he was done.

All of the participants had passed, a few squeaking by on the written, but all of them had excellent practical skills. The only thing left for Cameron to do was to pack up the paperwork. But even though he would rather see what Noah had in mind for dinner—and maybe if he had something in mind before dinner—Cameron helped the facility's lifeguard store away the equipment, because that's what Havers employees did.

Noah worked alongside him, gathering up rescue tubes and stripping the dummies for cleaning.

"You said you turned the acid up?" the teenaged lifeguard asked.

"Yeah, the pH was eight point three. I'll turn it back. And retest it." He smiled and forced the sigh back into his stomach. More delays. Well, it wasn't as if they could hit the beach; rain had swept in again.

Cameron was able to walk into the pump room to grab the test tubes, to go back to the pool for a sample, but as soon as he stepped back inside that small room—the sounds, the smell. God, he could feel Noah's mouth, the wet suction, the velvet of his throat as Cameron had fucked deep between those soft lips. He'd barely dropped the tablets in the test tubes before he got hard so fast he was dizzy. *A bit of a problem in their line of work?* No shit. He couldn't have this problem every time he came into a pump room. And just now *came* was the totally wrong word to use. He turned back the acid and shook the test tubes, crowding against the shelf as the kid came over to ask what the reading was.

"Seven point six," Cameron said without turning around. "And the free chlorine is two point oh." His voice was steadier than he could have hoped considering his balls had taken over his brain. People were going to think he had a jones for pump rooms.

Cameron took as long as he could to rinse out the test tubes.

"You know, you've got to come out of there sometime."

He looked over his shoulder. Noah was alone.

"Fuck you. It's all your fault. Where's the kid?"

"Locking up the gear. Now's your chance to"—Noah tipped his head—"limp to the locker room for a cold one."

God, the brat had gotten too damned sure of himself. But with that build and that mouth and that ass, he had every reason. Cameron moved as quickly as he could to grab his sweatshirt from the bag. "I'm going to just head back to the hotel."

Noah looked all of fifteen again. Cameron read the hurt and confusion in the hunch of those broad shoulders, the lowering of Noah's bright gaze.

"Oh, okay. I—uh checked out of my room this morning. So…"

"I promised you breakfast," Cameron said.

Noah straightened. "Yeah, you did."

"I just have to get my paperwork, and I'm out of here. You

know where the Majestic is?"

"I can find it."

"Room 735."

Noah's dimples ought to come with some kind of warning label. Cameron was already hard enough to hit one out of the park with it, and now with Noah smiling like that, it took all Cameron's self-control to keep from fucking him up against the lifeguard stand.

"Seven thirty-five," Noah repeated and headed into the locker room.

∿∿

As it turned out, Noah was ready for dinner when he showed up, dressed in khakis and that same blue-striped shirt Cameron had wanted to rip off yesterday.

"I'm starving. What kind of meal allowance do you get anyway?" Noah asked.

They ate at the hotel's casual restaurant, more of a pub. They didn't talk about Adam, or the Yankees' pitching staff, or growing up in Pensacola, but three hours had passed before Cameron realized it, and he really didn't remember what they'd talked about, just that it was getting harder to reconcile the Noah sitting across the table, stealing the last French fry from Cameron's plate, with the kid he'd known before. He finished his beer, and they settled the bill before heading up to the room in comfortable silence.

They still weren't talking when they got in the room, mouths too busy kissing once the door had closed behind them. It was slower this time, as if they'd burnt away the urgency that afternoon.

Noah's hands moved with smooth heat and pressure under Cameron's shirt, down the front of his pants, back up, never stopping the deep languid strokes with his tongue. Cameron popped the fly on Noah's khakis and slid underneath to cup his ass through the cotton of his briefs. Noah pressed harder against Cameron's dick, and he let Noah's mouth go long enough to steer them to the bed. With them stretched out, Cameron didn't have to pull Noah's head down or go up to meet him. Cameron could just press his weight against the long stretch of hard muscle everywhere beneath him. He wanted it to be nothing but warm skin, and he jerked off his shirt, tugged at Noah's.

The laziness was disappearing under a crushing wave of need. Skin to skin wasn't going to be enough; Cameron had to be in Noah. Now.

"If you don't want to have to replace the buttons, get this off." Cameron sat up and straddled Noah.

Noah grinned and yanked the shirt over his head.

Maybe later Cameron would fuck Noah over the desk with that shirt on, because the thought of watching those shoulders under blue stripes as he bucked back Cameron's thrusts made every drop of blood stop what it was doing and rush down to join the fun.

He leaned in to kiss him again, hands holding Noah's cheeks as Cameron's thumbs stroked the stubble on that sharp-edged jaw. Noah opened to Cameron's kiss, to the press of his body, knees bracketing Cameron's hips as he ground down into him. Noah's hands rubbed the back of Cameron's neck, kneaded the base of his spine, urging him closer. *Fuck!* Why hadn't he undressed them standing up?

Noah tipped his hips up, and their goddamned pants were no longer tolerable. Cameron rolled them on their sides, shoving at Noah's waistband. Noah wriggled free, his hands unzipping Cameron without bothering about the button, and Noah's hand dove inside.

There was nothing left of those slow kisses now. Cameron gasped into Noah's neck. "Shit. Just, God, Noah, let me—" But Noah's hand didn't stop.

Cameron worked his own pants off his hips so fast he was afraid he was going to damage something really important, and then finally there was nothing but skin between them. He pulled Noah back underneath him. A wet kiss from Noah's cock head brushed Cameron's hip as he moved his mouth to Noah's neck, licking and nipping to his ear. He sighed as Cameron wrapped one hand around their cocks and one hand in Noah's long, soft hair.

Noah caught the rhythm right away, sliding against Cameron's cock so the rims clicked against each other as they rubbed up and down. Cameron tightened his grip in Noah's hair, watched the dark red stain spread on Noah's exposed throat before licking over his Adam's apple and down to the notch at the bottom. Noah started to make that whimper again, the one he'd made when Cameron had sucked Noah off, when Cameron had been deep in Noah's ass.

That sounded like a really good plan right about now.

One last kiss, one last stroke of their dicks together, and Cameron shifted off Noah and onto his hip, reaching for the lube in the nightstand. "Roll over, babe."

"No."

Cameron looked down at Noah. "No?"

But before Cameron's mind could come up with a reason for the sudden shift, Noah said, "You want to fuck me? Okay. But we do it face to face."

Cameron hesitated. What the hell difference did it make

67

how they fucked? All right. He'd admit he had a bit of a dominant streak that got off on holding a guy on his stomach or knees as he pounded into him, but it wasn't as if he always had to do it that way. His dick didn't really care as long as it was getting squeezed in smooth, tight heat. So why was something in his gut telling him this was a bad idea? The rest of him strongly disagreed. His hips, his thighs, even the muscles of his ass burned with the need to finish this. Now. Inside Noah.

"Pushy," Cameron said with a smile he didn't quite feel. "Okay, babe." His thumb popped the cap on the lube.

"And don't call me that."

"Huh?"

"Babe. I don't like it."

"And I don't really like being called Cam."

"Fine." Noah sounded exasperated.

It was getting awkward enough to make his dick wilt. "So can we fuck now? Or is this going to be more complicated than Middle East peace negotiations?"

"You're the one with the lube, man." Noah grinned up at him and dragged a pillow down under his hips.

"Just for that I'm not warming this up." Cameron rubbed the gel across his fingers and slid two into him.

Noah jumped at the first contact. "Fuck, that's cold."

"Serves you right, pushy brat."

Noah pressed down onto Cameron's fingers, eyes squeezed tight.

Cameron brought his other hand up to stroke Noah's dick. "Something wrong?"

"Just..." he panted, "...different like this."

Cameron twisted his wrist, the balls of his fingers

searching, rubbing. The shift in Noah's expression would have told Cameron even if he couldn't feel the swelling beneath his fingers.

Noah's head dropped back against the pillows. His hips bucked up as Cameron kept up that press, not even fucking, just stroking over and over until Noah was making that whimper he loved hearing, the sound so incongruous from his deep chest.

"Fuck me, Cam—er—on."

It sounded ridiculous. "Just Cam," he sighed and rolled his eyes.

"C'mon," Noah urged. His eyes had gone dark, pupils blown wide with arousal, but no less intense as they focused on his.

Cameron rolled down the rubber. Holding Noah's thigh open with one hand, Cameron used the other to guide himself in. Noah's muscles clamped down around the head. His hand came up to rest against Cameron's chest. It wasn't precisely shoving him away, but it wasn't exactly welcoming either. Cameron knew they'd gone too fast.

"Noah?"

Noah's hand slid down around Cameron's waist and pulled him forward. "Yeah. S'all right."

But it didn't feel all right. Cameron had fucked enough guys to know when things were a little too tight for fun and things were more than a little too tight right now. It was like being crushed in a fist. A hot, slick fist.

"Noah. I—"

Noah lifted his hips off the pillow, and Cameron gained another inch. He reached for Noah's dick again, but Noah pushed Cameron's hand away.

"Noah, let me—"

Noah brought his knees up, and Cameron slid all the way home.

Noah's groan vibrated to Cameron's bones.

"Move," Noah panted.

Cameron flexed his hips, a long, slow withdrawal, and watched the sensations play across Noah's features. He felt the rim of muscle quiver and clench on his crown and sank all the way in again. No resistance now, just searing heat and perfect pressure the whole length of his cock.

"C'mon," Noah said again, thighs cradling Cameron's hips, body throbbing around Cameron's dick.

It felt so good every time a guy gave Cameron this, opened his body, yielded strength to strength and took him in. It couldn't be any different, so what the hell was that tensing in his gut about? Why did Cameron feel like the whole fucking world was shifting as he drove into Noah?

Noah's hips arched up to meet him on every stroke, and Cameron grabbed hold as he straightened up on his knees to slam into Noah hard and fast, pushing them into a long wave of pleasure that didn't give Cameron any time to think.

A line formed between Noah's brows, but his eyes stayed open, the pleasure and need so clear in them that Cameron felt that uncomfortable tug in his gut again. He leaned forward, his hand running through Noah's hair, tightening and pulling as Cameron lifted him into a kiss. Cameron slowed his thrusts, worked Noah in a slow, deep swivel, and Noah's slick cock pressed between their stomachs as Cameron held him.

He couldn't kiss him long. Neither of them had the breath for it. As soon as Noah's mouth was free, he groaned. "Need. Need to come, Cam."

Cameron went back to kissing him, hand soothing Noah's scalp from the yanking Cameron had given those silky strands.

"Yeah." Cameron pressed up against Noah's shoulders and then moved his hands to Noah's thighs, pinning him down, holding him open.

Noah's head lolled loose on his neck like Cameron had fucked through Noah's spine, and Cameron could feel himself sinking so far in he thought he might. He snapped his hips faster. Noah's fingers dug into Cameron's biceps, the pain helping him hang on as the sparks started going off in his balls. He slung one of Noah's legs over his shoulder and reached for Noah's cock, fingers sliding on sweat, lube and precome.

A few strokes and Noah was arching into Cameron's fist, hands pulling him closer, tightening until Cameron knew there'd be bruises. He jerked Noah's cock faster, trying to match the speed of his hips until Noah bucked and whined, those eyes finally slamming shut as he came.

His cries were just loud enough to hear over the rough smack of flesh as Cameron tried to fuck every last whimper out of Noah's throat, force every last shudder and spurt from his cock. Noah's hands fell away from his arms, and his eyes opened.

Cameron hit the point of no return. His hips thrust him forward so hard his balls ached from slamming into Noah's ass, and then stuttered as that electricity ripped through him, squeezed the breath from his lungs.

The last thing Cameron saw was that bright blue gaze through the mess of black bangs and then everything burst in a long flood of white heat pumping inside Noah. It seemed to go on forever, Noah's still-pulsing muscles milking his cock until Cameron just hung his head and dragged the breath back into his lungs. Aftershocks chased each other up and down his nerves. He fought exhaustion for a minute, and then collapsed onto Noah's come-slippery chest.

"God, you're hot when you come." Noah's voice rumbled in Cameron's ear.

"Oh?" He had to get rid of the rubber, but at the moment, he didn't think he could remember how many toes he had, and he certainly couldn't feel them.

"Yeah. Loved watching you," Noah said around a yawn.

Noah's heart was still pounding against Cameron's chest, breath still ragged, but Cameron could feel Noah drifting away. Noah was a hell of a lay, but he really overworked the roll-over-and-go-to-sleep cliché. Even if it was flattering to think Cameron had fucked the brat senseless. The idea made heat pool thick and slow and deep inside Cameron, as sweet as the satiation already turning his hips and thighs to lead.

Noah's eyes were already closed when Cameron managed to peel himself free and get up to toss the rubber in the toilet. By the time he got back to bed, Noah was dead to the world. On top of the comforter.

Cameron wiped down Noah's chest with a towel and managed to roll him—with mumbled complaints and very little help—onto the sheets.

"Your post-performance could use a little work." He told the back of Noah's head and propped himself up against all the pillows.

～～
～～

The room was dark when Noah woke up, his heart slamming into his ribs as he tried to sort out where he was. The warmth of another body seeping into his made the tension and confusion drain away. He turned his head. Cam was sleeping beside him, sprawled on his back, one arm flung over his head.

He'd stolen all the pillows. And God help him, Noah thought that was cute, despite his stiff neck.

Noah couldn't resist running his hand down the length of Cam's torso, sleep-warm skin tingling his palm as he stroked the muscles and ridges. Cam shifted, but didn't wake. The tingle spread up Noah's arm as he brushed his thumb over Cam's nipple. With a sleepy grunt, Cam grabbed Noah's forearm and tugged him closer, turning on his side and pulling Noah around him like a blanket. And let Noah share a pillow.

♒

When Noah woke again, it was light and he was alone. He didn't hear the shower running. He sighed, looked down at the bruises on his knuckles and aimed the punch at the pillow. Paper crunched on impact.

Noah smoothed it out. At least Cameron had left a note this time.

Went for a swim. What do you want for breakfast?

Noah smiled and rolled out of bed. His morning wood was thinking blowjobs in the shower would make a nice breakfast. He pushed open the curtains and looked down at the green waters of the Gulf. A couple of dots moved between the white rows of waves. He stretched and checked his watch. Nine thirty. He had a class to teach in Tallahassee at five. He wondered what time Cam's flight was.

The door opened.

"Man, Noah, you really like your sleep. I tried to wake you up."

Drying salt sparkled in Cam's hair, across his tan shoulders. He peeled off his tank top in the hall and stepped into the bathroom. A second later, the shower started.

Noah followed, driven by his bladder as much as his wish to see Cam. Of course, first the sight of Cam sparkly from his swim and now the outline of him on the other side of that translucent curtain weren't helping Noah get his erection to subside enough to give his bladder relief.

He'd almost gotten soft enough to offload his kidneys when Cam spoke.

"So where are we going for breakfast?" Cam's voice sounded raspy, probably from the salt water, but Noah's dick thought it sounded like sex.

He muttered "Fuck" under his breath before he said out loud, "I don't know. How's the other restaurant here?"

Maybe if he could focus on food and not a dripping wet naked Cam…if he could think about how hungry he was, how much he needed a cup of coffee…

"I saw a place that looked good a couple blocks away. We could walk. The guy at the hotel desk said they have huge omelets."

Omelets weren't sexy, thank God. He remembered not to flush and then pulled open the curtain. "I like omelets."

Cam moved so he could slide in. "You need to be anywhere today?"

"I have to leave by two." Noah ducked under the spray.

"I need to leave for the airport by one."

The matter-of-fact schedule, the sudden realization that their time was measured in hours, left Noah feeling a lot less hungry. *You knew this was going to be it. Don't turn into some whiny bitch over it.* He shook the water out of his hair.

"Goddamn, what are you, part Saint Bernard?" Cameron wiped at his eyes.

Noah hung out his tongue in an imitation of a panting dog.

"Hmm." Cam leaned in and drew Noah's tongue into his mouth.

Noah's skin buzzed. The need for one more—*God, just once more*—hummed in his bones.

Cam must have had the same idea, since his soapy hand zeroed in on Noah's half-hard dick and dealt with that *half* nonsense pretty much instantaneously.

"You sore?" Cam murmured into his mouth.

"Not at all."

Cam yanked the curtain aside and dug into his shaving stuff, coming back with a condom between his teeth and a grin that made Noah's balls tighten.

Noah's extra couple of inches in height lined them up perfectly. His fingers splayed out against the tile. He'd never been fucked standing up, and he wasn't sure his legs were going to hold him. Cam rocked their bodies together as Noah's insides just melted, hot and slow. He wanted it to last, but everything was wet and slick, Cam's arm around Noah's waist, soapy smooth hand on his dick, water rushing between them as Cam shifted and arched deeper.

"Cam—"

"Don't, babe. Noah, wait, please. Wanna finish you in my mouth."

His legs were shaking as Cam moved them faster. Nails going deep into the tile and grout, Noah clamped his ass around Cam's short, tight thrusts.

"Yeah. Fuck, babe that's—"

Cam's hips jerked, his grip squeezing around Noah's waist, and he had never wanted more to feel this with just skin, to feel the flood of heat inside him. Noah leaned back so that his head could rest on Cam's shoulder as Cam shuddered through his orgasm, his mouth lapping at the water on Noah's neck.

When Cam spun Noah back into the spray and dropped to his knees, Noah had to tighten his muscles before he lost it from the first brush of Cam's lips. Cam looked up at him, and Noah's legs shook again. Rimmed with water-spiked lashes, those green eyes studied his face as Cam slowly sucked him down.

It was the last time, and Noah needed to hold on, just make it last a little longer, but Cam hummed around Noah's cock, and it wasn't fucking fair. His back slid down the tiles. Cam slipped his fingers down behind Noah's sac and pushed inside, pressing forward. Noah's balls hiked up into his body as he fought the rush toward that peak. Cam's tongue flickered over the head while his fingers rubbed hard, and Noah's spine came unglued as he exploded into Cam's mouth. Noah's mind blanked out.

When his brain decided to come back, he found himself squatting against the wall, Cam's steadying hands the only thing keeping them both from tumbling out through the curtain. Noah looked down at Cam's come-shiny lips, dick twitching again. And God Noah wished it was only his dick. Because looking down at Cam and knowing it was the last time sat like a big lump of clumpy oatmeal in the back of Noah's throat, and he had no idea how he was supposed to go out for omelets and wave good-bye now that he knew, *knew* how good they were together.

What the fuck else was there to do? He could just see Cam's face if Noah yanked the guy into his arms to say he couldn't stand the idea of never seeing Cam again. That Noah couldn't let Cam disappear from his life this time. Cam would run faster than he had after Adam's wedding. So somehow Noah was going to have to sit across from him and choke down breakfast and pretend that it didn't feel like drowning to have to watch him leave.

Noah ran his fingers through the wet curls on Cam's head. Catching Noah's hand, Cam wove their fingers together as he got them both back on their feet. After ducking under the spray to rinse his mouth, Cam leaned in and kissed him, holding Noah tight as the water beat down on them. Noah had felt sure Cam would be pushing him away a lot harder. Maybe they could figure out a way to see each other again. No, that would be too much to ask for.

Cameron pulled back with a gentle suck on his lower lip. "Check out's at eleven."

"Yeah."

And there really wasn't anything left to do but dress and go to breakfast.

Chapter Four

Noah kept Cam's business card on the phone table for three weeks. Cam had slid it across the table at Eggscetera with a murmured, "Keep in touch." Noah had relayed his own number and watched Cameron type it into his phone. Not that Cam had used it. Neither of them had. Noah hadn't even bothered to transfer the number on the card into his cell.

He had checked the Havers website to see where Cam was headed. Indiana, Missouri, New Jersey. But Noah stopped checking after the first week. Because it didn't matter where Cam was since he wasn't here, wasn't going to be here, and when Noah got home tonight he was going to throw out the business card. He dismissed his water safety class a little before seven and stepped into the pool office.

His cell had a voice mail.

The bitterness that had soured everything in the last three weeks disappeared in a rush of optimism as he saw that North Carolina area code. The first time through he didn't hear much except that it was Cam's voice, so Noah replayed the message.

"I'm doing an inspection in White Water Park in Panama City next week. Got any plans for Sunday?"

Noah's thumb hovered over the call back button. And then he hit a speed dial number instead. He needed help.

~~~
~~~

When Joey walked into the coffee shop, both male and female eyes watched him make his way to the table where Noah was waiting. It might have been the purple and white streaks in his hair, but Noah knew otherwise. Joey was just one of those people who everyone wanted to meet. As soon as you saw him, you knew he was going to make you smile.

Joey leaned on Noah's table, hands splayed to show that the alternating colors on his fingernails matched the dye in his hair. "Is it so much of an emergency I can't get a macchiato?"

"I never said it was an emergency."

"Not out loud. But honey, your voice was screaming 911."

Sometimes Noah hated how perceptive Joey was, but that was why Noah had called his ex-boyfriend. It'd been more than a year since Joey had broken up with Noah and moved out, and Joey was still Noah's best friend. "Get your coffee. I promise not to meltdown in the next five minutes."

Joey's warm brown eyes swept him from head to toe before he left him to get in line at the counter. Noah tried to figure out how to bring this up. He and Joey had fought over Cam once, early on. Sharing coming-out stories had turned into Joey accusing Noah of being emotionally unavailable because he was waiting for Prince Cameron to ride up and carry him off. Noah had hotly denied it. Now he was afraid that, like Joey was about everything else, he had been right.

Joey slid his mug onto the table and dropped into the chair across the table.

"Thanks for coming."

Joey waved that off. "Shut up and get to it. We've only got

two hours before they close. So. How's Cameron?"

A latte really burned when it came back out through your nose. "Jesus. How the fuck do you do that?" Noah asked.

"You really don't want to know."

"Yes, this time I think I do."

Joey sighed and ran his finger down the side of the mug. "Okay. I call and invite you to a party and you can't make it because you've got Havers training and instead of the usual way you talk about it, like you've got your execution coming up, you sound all excited. So I call Donna—"

"You called the athletic director's secretary?"

"I told you you didn't want to know. I always liked Donna. Anyway, I call Donna and ask about the recertification and she reads off the instructor's name. Then you come back and don't call for three weeks until I get this breathless, desperate, completely un-Noah-like voice begging me to meet him for coffee." He spread his hands. "It was your Cameron, wasn't it?"

"Yeah." The word echoed in Noah's mug as he tried to hide behind it. Leave it to Joey to take care of the awkward how-do-I-bring-this-up part.

"And you fucked."

More latte leaked out of his nose. He pushed his mug far away.

"How was it?"

"Joey."

"Do you want my help with this or not?"

"Yes." Joey was the only person Noah knew who might be able to help him figure out Cam.

"So how was the sex?"

Noah grabbed for the shield of his mug again. Talking

about sex with someone else you'd had sex with was seriously fucking awkward.

"Don't make me get the dolls."

Noah looked up in alarm, half-afraid Joey would produce the dolls he used with the abused teens and kids he counseled when they couldn't use words. The idea of showing Joey was suddenly way worse than telling him.

"You bottomed, didn't you?"

Noah nodded.

Joey's grin turned absolutely lascivious. "How big is he?"

Noah wanted to crawl into his mug. "Nine inches," he mumbled.

Joey's eyebrows waggled. "Now you know how lucky I felt."

"Oh, don't even tell me you're not still lucky. Mark is huge."

Joey licked his lips and his tongue ring flashed. Sometimes Noah really missed that tongue ring.

"I'll make it easy for you, hon. I'll tell you what happened." Joey took a long sip. "He panted after you and you felt like you were fifteen again and he fucked you on your knees every time and wouldn't let you suck him off."

How the hell did Joey do that? "Not exactly." Noah swirled the latte around. "He—I made—we did it face-to-face once."

"Really? And?"

"He was gorgeous."

"Besides that."

Noah closed his eyes. "He wouldn't look at me at first. And then—"

"Did he kiss you?"

"Yeah." Cam's hips grinding slow and deep, the press of his sweaty skin, tongue fucking as deep as his cock.

"Hmm."

"God, do you have to make those clichéd therapist sounds?"

"Yes." Joey's smile was smug.

"And I did suck him off." Noah glanced around in embarrassment as he realized he'd said that a lot louder than the rest of their conversation, but no one was looking at them in shock so he just continued in a lower tone. "It was a rush job, but—"

"Get him all?"

"Everything but the last inch."

"He got your throat around him, and he let you go? He's insane."

"He called. He's coming to see me Sunday."

"Ahh."

Noah rolled his eyes.

"So now we get to the real reason you called me." Joey fixed a stare on him, and Noah knew how Joey could get the most defiant teenager to sit down and shut up. "And no bullshit, Noah. You've been in love with the idea of Cameron for half your life. You had your do-over. Is that all you wanted?"

Noah's latte had gotten cold but he drank it down anyway. "No."

"You want *this* Cameron. Not some ideal."

"Yeah."

"Things aren't going to change if you keep falling into the same patterns."

Joey was right, as usual.

"How did I ever put up with all this therapist psychobabble for more than a year?"

"Because I also have a hot ass."

"True. So what? Tell him no?"

"No. I'm not saying you should play some kind of cat-and-mouse game with him. I'm saying change things up. Don't let him have everything his way. Part of him still sees you as the kid you were. He has to see you as an equal or it's never going to work."

"You can't be more specific?"

"Bring him to brunch," Joey said.

"What brunch?"

"The brunch I've just decided Mark and I are hosting in honor of your birthday. This Sunday."

"At your place." The sinking feeling in Noah's stomach had nothing to do with a cold latte.

"That's what hosting means, honey."

"Yeah, but—"

"If Cameron won't even come with you, you've got your answer."

"It's not that, it's—"

"What?"

"You know your boyfriend scares me a little."

Joey grinned and pushed his tongue ring between his teeth. "Me too," he said with a happy sigh. "So, bring Cam along and I'll tell you what I think." Joey tipped back his mug.

"Thanks, Joey."

Joey leaned in and kissed him, just deep enough for Noah to feel the brush of that silver stud on Joey's tongue. It was familiar and it was sweet, but it wasn't Cam. And then there was the image of Mark, with his huge tattooed arms. Noah pulled back.

"Anything for the guy who broke my heart." Joey tilted his head and gave a sad smile.

"You moved out, remember?"

"Doesn't mean you didn't break my heart." Joey stroked his fingers along Noah's jaw and left.

∽∽∽

When he called Cam back, Noah said that he'd already committed to the brunch, but didn't mention anything about his birthday. He was afraid that would make him sound desperate for some sort of acknowledgement. Cam said he wouldn't mind going to the brunch. At nine on Saturday night, Noah got the text: "Wear the blue-striped shirt."

A bubbly, hopeful feeling jolted Noah awake at six-fifteen Sunday morning. A feeling like Christmas or a trip to Disney World, way better than just his birthday should feel. He covered his face with his hands. It wasn't just his birthday; Cameron was coming.

And he was far too excited about it.

He wrapped his head in pillows and tried to fall back asleep, but that feeling kept squirming beneath his diaphragm, cutting off the deep breaths necessary to slide back under where he belonged.

He wasn't expecting Cam until around ten, so when the door buzzed at nine, Noah wasn't ready. He yanked the shirt over his head and raked a hand through his hair as he hurried to the door.

Cam was there, on *his* doorstep and the look he gave Noah made his throat tighten.

"I drove fast."

Noah stepped back, and Cam pushed in, tossing a bag on the table by the door. He backed them up until Noah's hips hit the couch.

"You didn't get the second part of my text?"

"Which was?" Noah's voice was a lot steadier than he'd thought it could be.

"The part about not wearing pants." Cam's thumbs were already easing under the waistband of Noah's sweats.

"Missed that one."

Cam crowded him until Noah started to lose his balance, and he reached out to grab Cam's shoulders. Cam used the leverage to kiss him, hard and deep. Noah'd felt the pulse in his cock from the minute the door buzzed, and now it started to throb. Cam's hands slipped lower, slid around behind Noah and yanked him close.

Cam's dick was a steel pike against Noah's own, and Noah matched Cam's hard-on faster than his next breath. The blood rushed down so fast it hurt, like a twist on Noah's balls.

"Can we skip all the how've-you-beens? Because I've been hard since I got in the car this morning." Cam's breath teased across Noah's lips.

Noah knew this was what Joey had been telling him about. Now was the time to put on the brakes, to stop giving in to everything Cam suggested. And what was the point of calling Joey if Noah wasn't going to listen to him? But this was every fucking wet dream come true. Cam wanting him, need burning in those green-gold eyes. Cameron Lewis so desperate for him they weren't going to make it to the bed. It was the best birthday present Noah could think of.

"Yeah." He could listen to Joey on a day not his birthday.

Cam spun Noah around until he was bent over the back of

the couch. One hand slid the sweats from Noah's ass. The other dove between Noah's legs and found his cock. "God, Noah, I need to fuck you. Please."

He knew Cam never begged, never needed anyone like this. The hoarse desperation in Cam's voice as he finger-fucked Noah open filled that bubble in Noah's chest again. He might have been the one with his ass in the air, but as Cam panted, "Ready? God, please, tell me," in Noah's ear he'd never felt more in control.

"Yeah."

Noah wasn't ready. They were both in too much of a hurry, but it didn't matter. Noah knew that blinding pressure, that sting was going to give way to pleasure so sharp and deep Noah would never want to come back from it. Cam's hand snaked around Noah's hips, lube-slick fingers finding the right stroke on his cock. That flicked a switch inside him. His muscles gave, sucked Cam all the way in.

"God, babe, so good, so good for me."

Cam's hand found Noah's where he clutched the top of the couch and laced their fingers together. Noah was driving back as hard as Cam was slamming forward and it was too fast, their bodies racing to the finish. It was always too fast. Noah could have this for an hour, and it would still be over too fast.

"Please, Noah, God, I can't—"

Cam was losing control—Cameron Lewis calm and so goddamned smug was falling apart from fucking him and nothing had ever felt better.

Their fingers tightened around each other. Noah felt the explosion build. Waiting. Almost. Just—

"Come for me, please, babe."

A hard twist, a harder thrust, Cam's growl in Noah's ear,

and he shot hard enough that he thought he lost some spinal fluid with it. Cam squeezed Noah's hand so tight his bones ground together as Cam jerked and shuddered and groaned.

They ended up on the floor, panting, sweaty and sticky. Cam finally rolled away.

"Here." Cam picked up the plastic bag he'd brought and put it on the floor next to him. "Happy Birthday."

Noah opened the bag and his mouth watered at the scent of super sour candy. And his stomach warmed with the knowledge that Cam had remembered the date and bought something.

"The lady in the candy store said it was the sourest stuff she had," Cam said. "I remembered there wasn't anything too sour for you as a kid. Adam and I couldn't believe the crap you ate."

Goddamn Joey for being right. Again. Cam was never going to stop thinking of Noah as a kid. The realization didn't stop him from popping one of the thickly coated worms into his mouth.

♒

Noah knew Cameron could be charming when he wanted to be, but Noah had forgotten the effect that charm could have on other people. He wanted to spend half his time at the brunch puffing his chest out with pride and the other half draping himself over Cam to mark his territory.

Joey's parties usually started at a minimum of twenty people, so Noah was glad there were only about a dozen guys out on Joey and Mark's deck. And he couldn't fault Cam's behavior—even Joey couldn't have found fault with Cam's behavior. He scored major boyfriend points by bringing Noah a mimosa and then stood hip to hip with him as they leaned against the railing to eat.

When Cam was distracted by something, Joey flashed him a sympathetic you-are-so-screwed look and pantomimed calling him.

Joey didn't know what the fuck he was talking about. Noah had never had a better birthday.

They had sex again when they got back to Noah's, Cam insisting that receiving a blowjob was a necessary part of birthday celebrations.

Noah was flopped back onto the bed, trying to get his heart rate down to something under exploding-out-of-his-ears fast when Cam said, "Your friend's kind of protective of you."

He was going to kill Joey. When had he found time to corner Cam? "Yeah, um, we used to go out."

"He's your ex?" Cam sounded surprised.

"Yeah, why?"

"No reason."

But there was a reason. Noah could hear it in the strange tightness in Cam's voice.

"Want me to take care of that?" Noah looked down at Cam's hard dick.

"Maybe."

Noah could still hear that edge to Cam's voice, as if there was something he didn't want to say. Maybe he was mad. Cam couldn't be jealous of Joey. So what was going on?

Intent on licking his way down Cam's chest, Noah leaned over Cam. He caught him by the biceps and rolled him under, arching so that his rigid cock slid against Noah's soft, sensitive one. Noah winced, and Cam shifted higher so that he rocked against the stretch of Noah's sweaty stomach.

Bracing his hands wide on the bed, Cam released Noah's arms and ground down. Cam's eyes were closed.

Noah's day went from perfect to sucking in nine point two seconds. Far be it for him to deny a guy a good time, but he wasn't some anonymous piece of flesh to rub off on.

"Cam. Cameron."

Cam groaned and kept rocking.

Noah hooked Cam's leg and flipped them.

Cam's face got even more distant. "What?"

Noah climbed up until his ass rubbed against Cam's dick. Cam sank his teeth into his lower lip.

"Fuck me."

"Noah..."

What the hell had changed since this morning—hell, since five minutes ago?

Noah could just reach the nightstand drawer and keep his ass in contact with Cam's dick. After fishing out the lube, he tore a condom off the strip.

Cam raised himself up on his elbows. "Noah." If Cam was going to be using that tone, Noah'd rather hear *babe*.

Noah tossed the lube and condom onto Cam's chest and got Cam's dick cradled in the crease of his ass. "Fuck me," Noah repeated, tightening his ass on him.

Cam fell back with a groan. Noah squeezed again, shifting up and down.

"Why?" Cam asked.

Noah pressed up on Cam's shoulders. He couldn't have been more surprised if Cam had grown tits. "What the hell? Because it feels good. Because I like it. Why else?"

"Really?" Cam's eyes narrowed and for a second everything

was back the way it was supposed to be. "Prove it."

"Huh?"

"Prove you want it. Show me."

If Cam had said that with a hint of his usual purr, Noah would have been slicking himself in a second. But there was still that hollow echo in Cam's tone. And suddenly Noah felt like it was some kind of job interview.

Noah swung off Cam, rolling to his back.

"So what? Now you're not interested?"

"Fuck you."

Cam gave a half-smile before he spun away to put his feet on the floor. "Or not." He pushed off the bed and stalked into the bathroom across the hall. The door closed. The shower started.

How could everything go to shit so fast? Noah's throat got tight like he was going into anaphylactic shock. Nothing had happened, so why the shift in Cam's mood? Noah had never seen Cam act like this before. Cam was arrogant, sexy and too fucking smug for his own good, but never bitchy. Noah took his forearm from his eyes to stare at the closed door. If Cam thought it was up to Noah to decipher that freaky mood swing, Cam deserved to be stuck in the shower with nothing but his own hand for company.

Noah checked the clock as he dragged himself off the bed. Three thirty, the Yankees game would be almost over. He went to the fridge, controlled the impulse to dump out the six pack of Corona he'd bought for Cam, and ordered nuclear hot wings and two Italian subs from Georgie's. It was Noah's birthday, and if Cam didn't like hot wings or salami, he could goddamned well order his own food.

When Cam came into the living room, the post game show

was on, and Cam was dressed in the khaki shorts and polo shirt he'd worn to the brunch.

Cam folded his arms across his chest and leaned against the doorframe. Noah didn't need Joey's help to decipher Cam's body language.

"Do you want me to leave?"

Noah thought about lying for half a second, and the truth still came out. "No." He wasn't angry anymore, just confused.

The door buzzed. Cam looked at Noah as he kicked away from the coffee table.

"Food," he answered Cam's raised eyebrow.

"I got it." Cam dug out his wallet.

Noah couldn't see what Cam handed the delivery guy but the effusive thanks at Cam's "Keep the change" made Noah hope his next delivery would be really speedy. Of course, Cam doling out a huge tip made Noah feel like Cam was apologizing to the delivery guy instead of to him. And Noah still didn't know what the hell had happened.

Noah took the bags and carried them to the coffee table. Cam stood in front of the sofa, brows raised. Other than a not particularly comfortable chair donated by his parents, the sofa was the only furniture to sit on in his apartment.

"So this is what your couch looks like from the front," Cam said at last.

Noah kicked him in the calf, and Cam sat down heavily.

"What'd you get?" Cam opened a bag and sniffed. Then waving a hand in front of his watering eyes, he asked, "Napalm?"

Chapter Five

Noah was surprised to wake up with a hot mouth on his dick. They'd gotten into his bed acting like straight guys forced to share a tent while camping, so waking up to Cam sucking him off was unexpected. And hot. And then too hot.

"Shit." He dug into Cam's hair and pulled him off.

"What?"

"Your mouth. The wings. Jesus. It's still got pepper on it or something."

Cam laughed. "There's a price to be paid for making me eat food that should be considered a fire accelerant."

"I didn't make you eat them."

Cam licked at Noah's inner thigh. What had been too much on his dick felt good and tingly there.

"But you ordered them." Cam was back to his sexy growl, and everything was comfortable again. He got up on his knees, an intent look on his face. "I wonder..."

His mouth fastened on one of Noah's nipples. The burn there was so perfect it had Noah arching up around Cam's body.

"Yeah. That's what I was wondering." Cam's grin felt as good as his mouth. His teeth flashed in the dark as he bent and licked at Noah's other nipple until his toes curled.

He didn't want things to get all awkward again, but he wanted...he reached for the nightstand.

"Already got it."

Yes. Noah arched his neck as need sent sparks chasing along his nerves.

Cam nipped at Noah's neck before he straightened up. Noah let his legs drop open.

He shouldn't say anything, shouldn't risk going back to whatever had screwed things up before, but Cam's fingers were slicking him inside and his brain-mouth filter stopped functioning.

"Fuck me, please. God, I want it."

"I know." In Cam's hoarse voice, those words might have been the hottest thing Noah had ever heard.

Noah twisted away from Cam's fingers. "Now."

Cam didn't laugh. Didn't call him pushy. Just eased inside Noah with one long, slow stroke. Noah's body relaxed into that so-good stretch, already craving friction. Cam gave it to him, reared back and slammed into him. Noah dug his heels into the mattress and met every deep, hard thrust.

Cam's head went back. His hands gripped into Noah's hips, and Noah wanted Cam's thumbs to sink farther in, to leave their shape in purple on Noah's skin. He wanted Cam to go so hard Noah would feel Cam in his ass for a week, just so Noah would have something left of Cam when he took off tomorrow.

Cam slowed, thumbs rubbing softer circles on Noah's hipbones and leaned in to burn his lips with that spicy kiss.

The angle made Cam shift and swivel inside. Noah shuddered the first time his cock head rubbed hard over his prostate, and then Cam was hitting it with each stroke of his hips. Cam's hand slid through Noah's hair and lifted his head

93

to meet Cam's kiss.

Whenever Noah swore he was a blink from coming, that he'd go over from just that incredible splash of pleasure in his ass, Cam's angle shifted and the urgency faded. Then it built again, hotter, closer, until every inch of Noah's skin was too thin, too full of sensation. Cam was fucking into all the spaces inside, kissing, licking Noah's ear, his jaw, murmuring things Noah couldn't hear over the pounding of their bodies, the thump of the bed, his own heart in his chest.

Cam lifted his head until their foreheads were pressed together and panted against Noah's lips, moving slow and sweet. "Don't wanna stop. Wanna fuck you all night, babe."

The pleasure built back up, bigger, so big it was almost scary this time, like coming would be letting a freight train rip through him. And Noah still didn't want it to stop.

"Yeah, Cam."

But Noah loosened the fist he was pressing into Cam's back and started to reach for his own cock because Noah had to do something, if he didn't he was going to slide out of his skin.

Cam hooked Noah's legs up higher, and Noah stretched them over Cam's shoulders. Cam fucked right up into Noah's heart, and he couldn't breathe. He swung his hands up to grasp Cam's forearms, desperate for an anchor.

Now Cam was the one shaking against Noah, shuddering through slow rolling thrusts. Cam's eyes glittered in the dark as his eyelids fluttered. Noah's legs slipped in sweat and he tightened his grip, his fingers digging into the hard muscle. Every breath was filled with the smell of their bodies straining together.

No sprint this time, a mile swim, slow, steady power moving them to the finish. Cam's head dropped forward, and he kissed Noah through a dozen liquid strokes.

"Close?" Cam whispered against Noah's lips.

"Been close...since...started," he managed between thrusts.

Cam lowered one of Noah's legs, turning his hips a little, and Cam's dick slid against all new nerves, driving Noah right to the edge. Cam kissed him harder and then started jacking Noah in time with the pressure inside him, faster and faster, the strength of Cam's hips and legs pumping them both over.

Electricity surged, lit Noah up, and he hoped Cam could hold on for another few seconds. "Now. Don't stop. Can't." Noah's fingers tore into Cam's arms, and Noah came like he hadn't come for a week, spasm after spasm dragging the spurts from deep inside him.

Cam leaned down and gave Noah one last taste of his lips before Cam's hips moved like he was going for the gold in the hundred-meter butterfly, his whole body arching and snapping.

Exhaustion surged up, rolled Noah under like rough surf. He knew Cam left the bed and came back and that he'd pulled a sheet over them, but Noah couldn't seem to make any of his own muscles move. He didn't even care how sticky his chest was.

"Noah." Cam's voice was urgent as he grabbed at Noah's jaw. "Listen, man, I know how you like your sleep, but listen for a minute."

Noah tried. Really tried to concentrate on Cam's words.

"I'll probably be gone when you wake up. And..."

Noah was going to tell Cam that opening the pool for seven A.M. lap swim meant Noah would definitely be up, but it was just too much effort.

"And I don't know when I'll see you—might not see you—"

That yanked Noah free of his fucked-out lassitude. "Huh?"

"I don't know when I'll be in the area again. So."

Noah would say Cam was breaking up with him, but they'd never actually talked about anything.

"I'm...glad I got to see you again, Noah."

What the fuck was Noah supposed to say to that? Thanks for the memories? What the hell was going on now? He'd never had sex like that before in his life and it was what, a goodbye fuck?

Cam expected Noah to fall asleep. That wasn't going to happen for a long while now, but if he faked it he wouldn't have to figure out what Cam expected him to say.

"Hm-hmm." Noah rolled away on his side, controlling the wince at the shift of well-used muscles.

He lay there and listened to Cam's breathing, trying to make his own slow in an approximation of sleep. His mind was drifting, but his eyes were still wide and staring when he felt Cam's hand thread through his hair. Cam's fingers rubbed and lifted and let a wave drop; his warmth drifted closer.

For someone who'd just delivered a pretty good imitation of the don't-call-me brush-off speech, Cam was damned cuddly. Noah swore he wouldn't sleep, couldn't sleep, but with Cam's fingers sliding and soothing, his knee hot against Noah's ass, the next thing Noah knew it was dawn, and Cam was opening the bathroom door.

"Sorry," Cam whispered from the hall.

Noah sat up. Cam was wearing his glasses.

"I've got a site inspection in St. Augustine today. Long drive."

"Drive safely." There wasn't much else to say. Cam had eliminated the potential in *see you*, or *talk to you soon*.

"I will."

As Cam stood in the door, Noah counted his heartbeats—

not all that challenging since his pulse was slamming against the top of his skull. Three, four, five—

"Bye, Noah."

"Bye."

Noah buried his face in sheets that smelled like come and sweat and Cam.

$$\approx$$

A city a day should have been enough to keep Cameron busy. It always had been. Between trainings, site inspections, class reviews, there was always something to do. Cameron figured he saw his apartment about once a month from March to September. And he liked it that way.

It wasn't unusual for him to be checking in to see if there were spare assignments. He liked the travel, liked the work, but he'd never spent so much time trying to find jobs in Northwestern Florida. Before now, it had always been too close to a you-were-right-here-why-didn't-you-stop guilt trip from his parents. Noah should be another reason to avoid the area. But even though he shouldn't, he wanted to see the brat again.

God, Cameron had never realized how seriously Noah had taken his crush. Cameron didn't know why he hadn't seen it, why he'd thought they could just have fun. And then he'd seen Noah's ex-lover and realized exactly what Noah was willing to do to be with Cameron.

That guy had been such a perfect, adorable bottom that Cameron's fingers had itched to grab Joey's hips and bend him over the nearest surface. Cameron could almost always read a guy's preference in the way he held himself, but he'd gotten so used to thinking of Noah like that because of the Noah Cameron

97

knew as a kid. And now it was clear Noah was only letting Cameron top because of that crush.

The cursor blinked at him from his laptop screen and he logged off the Havers website. Few people were likely to cancel on a Florida job in the spring. August and September there'd be more openings to fill, but that was months away. Which still didn't matter, he told himself, because he wasn't looking for reasons to head to Northwest Florida even if every time he jerked off he ended up picturing how Noah looked when he came.

Okay, obviously Noah liked getting fucked, but Cameron doubted it was what Noah was used to, and he was bound to get tired of it. And Cameron wasn't only a top in bed. People thought he was easygoing, but that was because he always made sure everything went his way. Forcing Noah to accept some kind of role because he thought he had to to be with Cameron...

Fucking hell, he should have seen it. He did see it at the bar that afternoon, but he'd ignored it. Noah didn't give off a bottom vibe. Despite his long hair and apple-shaped, fuckable ass, Noah carried himself like a top, stood like one, crowded in and challenged like one, except around Cameron.

Maybe he should have let it all hit the fan when Noah was fifteen. Then Cameron wouldn't be in a hotel room in upstate New York with his dick throbbing because he couldn't stop thinking about the whimpers Noah made, the way he fucked back into Cameron, hard and strong.

And Cameron needed to get it under control, because the water park he was checking out tomorrow had just signed with Havers this year and that meant a full inspection—rescue and everything. He was traveling with a partner this time. Kurt was a nice guy, a few years older and happily married, but Cameron didn't think Kurt would appreciate it if Cameron walked around the hotel room hard—or spent half his time in the shower. Kurt was scoping out the gift shop for stuff for his kids. Cameron had a few minutes to get things to subside.

Not only was the middle of the Adirondack mountains a stupidly frigid place to stick a water park—and he didn't care if they said it got hot in July, Cameron was going to have to play victim in the water in May—but the middle of the Adirondacks also appeared to be at least two hours in any direction from a gay bar—so fucking Noah out of his head wasn't in the offing either.

He had a job in Atlanta in two weeks. That was only about four hours from Tallahassee. No.

He scrubbed his hand over his face. It was just...the décor in this hotel was getting on his nerves. Red and black plaid with moose outlines had to be the theme of a special room in hell, or he wouldn't be feeling so frustrated with this job. And unless he wanted to browse similarly faux rustic stores, there wasn't anything to do up here. But he still wasn't calling Noah.

Cameron reopened his laptop and checked the Havers website, checked his banking. After brief consideration, he forced himself away from the airline sites, because he didn't need to see what seats to Tallahassee were going for. His phone rang.

The Florida panhandle area code didn't mean it was Noah, and it wasn't Noah's cell number. It could have been any one of a dozen facilities in that area that Havers supervised.

But it was Noah.

"I've got a few questions that came up in my water safety class. I know I could look them up, but I forgot to do it last night and class is in about ten minutes."

As excuses to call went, that one wasn't bad. "Shoot."

"Did the policy change last year on grand mal seizures in diving wells?" Noah asked.

"Nope. Just keep them breathing air as best you can and get more advanced care."

"Okay. And what's the minimum length on a ring buoy line for pools?"

"Twenty yards." That was a good one. If Cameron didn't do so many site inspections he'd have had to look it up himself.

"Thanks."

Talking to Noah had seriously improved Cameron's outlook on the day. "That it?" He wondered if Noah would come up with a few more obscure questions to prolong the conversation.

"That covers it."

"When do your classes end?"

"Finals are this week and next. I'm giving the written in a few minutes."

Silence echoed in Cameron's ear for a second and then he gave in. "Got any plans for Thursday the twenty-fourth?"

"Why?"

"I'm going to be in Atlanta. I know it's a long drive..."

He listened to Noah's breath catch, then Noah's words came fast, as if he thought Cameron would change his mind.

"It's a workday, but I can take it off. There's nothing going on at the pool until the summer session starts."

"I'll probably be at the airport Radisson. I'll call you."

"Okay."

Cameron heard the door lock click open and wrapped things up. Maybe sometime when he didn't have a roommate he'd see if Noah liked phone sex. Cameron still didn't want to get in the water tomorrow, but he no longer felt like taking a sledgehammer to the fake logs making up the dresser.

In the Albany airport, he bought Noah a Yankees hat.

$$\text{\large\rm www}$$

At the end of June, Noah's vacation week coincided with the Yankees playing the Devil Rays in Tampa, so Cameron got them tickets. He had enough frequent flyer miles to make a side trip, and offered to buy Noah's plane ticket, too, but Noah said that with the time he'd spend going through security, he could drive down faster.

The Devil Rays were last in the majors, but they still managed to thrash the Yankees, who were on their third pitcher by the top of the fourth.

"Sorry," Cameron said as the Rays belted another triple.

"You arranged for the Yankees to lose? I'm impressed."

"Well, it could be a better game."

"I don't care as long as the manager leaves the starters in long enough for me to finish this chart I'm doing." Noah looked up, eyes narrowed, and went back to scratching on the score card from the program.

"What chart?" Cameron snagged a couple of pretzels from a vendor. They were sitting behind third base and like most Devil Rays games—even with the Yankees in town—seats were plentiful. He stuck his foot on the empty chair in front of him.

"When the game's on TV, you have to watch what they show you. Here you can watch what you want."

"And that is?"

"Look." Noah handed over the scorecard as the Yankees finally managed a third out. He hadn't filled in the lineup card the right way. There were cross outs all over it, but he had the nine regular Yankees starters in what appeared to be a random order. "See?"

"No."

"I've decided that their batting averages are inversely proportionate to the cuteness—or lack thereof—of their asses."

Cameron laughed and then choked on a piece of pretzel. He studied the guy in the on-deck circle. "I think you should switch three and four."

"They're only eight points apart anyway."

"The theory doesn't hold for him, though." Cameron nodded at the guy at the plate.

"No, definitely not."

"God, I would so fuck that ass." Cameron watched the Yankees' shortstop send a long foul into the seats.

"Hmm."

"You wouldn't?"

"Those arms, those eyes, those legs? I think I'd let him fuck me. I'd rather fuck that one." Noah pointed at the young center fielder.

Cameron had never been more grateful to watch the Yankees lose a game in the standings. Because otherwise they'd have been too focused on the game for this shit, and he really wanted to know. "You really don't have a preference: top or bottom?"

"It's all sex, it's all good. It depends on who I'm with." Noah's answer was matter-of-fact.

"But don't you—?"

Noah turned to face him. "You like blowjobs—getting them I mean, right? And you like fucking. Is one better than the other?"

"Depends."

"See. You wouldn't want to give up one for the other forever, right?"

So that was it. Noah didn't want to give up topping—not forever. Not that Cameron was about to ask Noah to.

"Have you ever"—Noah looked out at the players on the field and winked—"caught?"

Cameron flicked the salt from his pretzel. "Twice. Once drunk and once sober. I didn't think much of it."

"Hurt?"

"Not that, just…didn't feel right."

"Did you come?"

"No."

Noah grinned. "Bet I could make you come." He took a big bite of his pretzel.

A sudden wave of vertigo had Cameron gripping the chair, and it had nothing to do with the closed roof of Tropicana Stadium or the warm beer he'd finished last inning. He concentrated on removing every particle of salt from his pretzel until his head got back to the right location instead of floating three feet above his shoulders.

"You think so?" Cameron licked a piece of salt from his fingers. His thighs tingled. He did like to flirt. Even if this was never going to happen, Noah's cocky smirk was turning Cameron on.

"I know so."

"Too bad you'll never have the chance."

"Is that a challenge?"

"No. It's a fact." The buzzing in Cameron's nerves told him it was anything but fact. He had to do something to get this back on familiar footing. He pushed his foot off the seat and leaned into Noah to growl, "Besides, you'd miss my cock in your ass, wouldn't you, babe?"

Cameron could see the flush of arousal on Noah's cheeks, but Noah's voice was steady.

"Maybe." Noah leaned away. "I know one thing that's a fact." He stood. "I've got to piss."

"Me, too."

Noah put his hand on Cameron's shoulder. "If you follow me, we're gonna get arrested for public indecency."

When Cameron got back from the bathroom, Noah had popcorn and a soda. Since Noah hadn't gone an inning without getting something from a vendor, Cameron should be glad it wasn't cotton candy. The thought of Noah getting sweet and sticky was too much to handle in public.

Noah handed off the box. Cameron checked the score as he sat, 14-5 in the fifth. He grabbed a handful of popcorn, wondering what Noah would say if he suggested that they just go back to the hotel. He passed back the popcorn box, and Noah offered the soda.

"Did you ever notice how much like good sex baseball is?" Noah asked.

"What?" Cameron almost snorted soda out of his nose.

Noah winked at him from under the hat Cameron had bought. "You know, a slow build of tension with each pitch, each swing. The way it eases and builds again until, if you're lucky, it explodes."

"You are a seriously perverted guy." As if Cameron needed more ways to think about sex and Noah. Now Cameron wouldn't even be able to watch a game online.

"I'm surprised you like baseball, Cam."

"Why?" This had all the makings of the opening of an uncomfortable conversation. He wished they could go back to talking about sex.

"Not enough action for you. You seem to like being busy."

"What's wrong with that?" Defensive anger burned in Cameron's chest. As soon as he saw a guy more than twice, conversations always started to focus on his job. How it took up too much of his life.

"Nothing. I just would think you would like hockey or basketball more." There was no judgment in Noah's tone, just curiosity.

Cameron smiled. "I guess because baseball's like sex. Once the good tension's gone, it relaxes me."

Noah's gaze focused on Cameron's lips, and the southerly direction of blood flow began to stir up problems. Noah drifted closer. He was going to kiss him. In Tropicana Stadium. In front of the Yankees. And they'd probably end up on TV.

Cameron stood. "I think this game's pretty much over."

"You don't look very relaxed." Noah tilted his head back and looked up. His eyes were taking on an aquamarine shade from the seats around them.

"I'm working on that part," Cameron said.

Their hotel was right next to the stadium. Noah flipped over to the game when they got back to their room. But when Noah took Cameron's cock deep in that velvet throat, he really didn't care that they'd just missed an unprecedented ten-run come back in the eighth.

Cameron spent most of July in Pennsylvania and Ohio.

Half the time the sites were close enough to drive to, so he was either traveling, working or sleeping. He offered to buy Noah a ticket if he had a free weekend, but Noah said he had to be on call in case something happened at his pool.

Cameron told himself that was good, that Noah wasn't turning this into something it couldn't be. That didn't help when the sound of Noah's voice on the phone got Cameron achingly hard, and what he heard in Noah's voice when he said good-bye made Cameron want to fly down as soon as he hung up.

Maybe he was the one with the problem. He'd never wanted the summer season to be over sooner. Never had seen his job as something that kept him from doing what he wanted. His job had always been what he wanted.

And what did he want? Noah? Sex with Noah for sure. And what else? Cameron kept waiting for Noah's crush to burn itself out with prolonged exposure. Waited for that intensity to fade. But it didn't, and it just got harder and harder to walk away from it. He'd never seen himself getting wrapped up in someone for this long. He'd expected Noah would get bored—that Cameron would get bored. But Noah didn't seem to be, and Cameron wasn't. An unfamiliar frustration combined with the stench of Ohio's peculiar haze of acrid factories and decaying farms to gift Cameron with a nauseating headache. He spent the last two weeks of July convinced his temples were being squeezed in a vise.

Chapter Six

The steel band squeezing Cameron's temples tightened a few more notches as he hung up the phone in his room at the Quality Inn and Suites in Geauga Lake, Ohio. The tiny town might boast a state of the art water park, but it was seriously lacking in hotel facilities—and this hotel needed immediate remediation workshops in customer service. Neither charm nor arrogance had gotten through to the smiling manager. Cameron still didn't fucking care if the hotel was overbooked. He wanted the room he had reserved.

Calling this room a shoebox would be overgenerous. He had to turn sideways just to edge around the queen bed. The air conditioner made enough noise to drown out the semi idling under his window, and provided zero cool breathable air. The manager had cut his room rate in half, which would look great on his expense account, but wasn't going to do shit to help him sleep tonight.

He took a cold shower and stretched out on the sheets. There were way too many theme parks in Ohio. Who thought of Ohio as the vacation destination? If he got stuck with Ohio next year, he was going to try to talk his supervisor out of having to drive from spot to spot. At least then he wouldn't have to deal with that weird smell.

When his cell buzzed and skittered across the nightstand, he really thought about ignoring it. It was probably Paul, telling Cameron about one more stop he had to make before he could get the hell out of Ohio.

But it was Noah. Cameron still thought about letting it go to voice mail. Noah hadn't done anything to deserve Cameron's bad mood, and he wasn't sure he could put on some kind of cheerful show, even for Noah.

Cameron hit answer anyway. "Hey."

"Hi." The size of Noah's chest gave his voice lots of room for reverberation. Cameron could have picked that deep voice out of a crowd. It was even deep enough to make him forget about the whines and groans coming from the ineffectual a/c.

Cameron tried to find something to say that wouldn't turn into a rant about the hotel, but even though his head felt a little better, he really didn't have anything to say.

"Where are you now?" Noah asked.

"Still in fucking Ohio."

"Ouch. No love for the Buckeye State?"

"I suppose I could be in Indiana—no wait, at least then I might not be at a Quality Inn."

"How low you have sunk. Did you piss off your booking agent?"

"It's all they've got." Cameron stared at the ceiling stained with orange water-damage rings.

"And now you're jonesing for the Radisson?"

"I'm jonesing for a little a/c." Cameron rolled off the bed and smacked the plastic. The whining stopped for a second, and then the motor grumbled, moaned and started whining about an octave lower.

"That sounds really primitive. Do they even have a

minibar?"

"Don't be a smartass."

"What did you say about my ass?"

Cameron could hear Noah's grin right through the phone. Flopping back on the bed, he asked, "Fishing for compliments?"

"Nah, I thought maybe you'd started phone sex and I missed it."

Not tonight, I have a headache. The cliché was almost out of Cameron's mouth before he realized his head didn't hurt anymore. "I thought you said your phone bill couldn't handle more."

"I said the phone couldn't handle it. I got lube all over it last time."

Cameron pictured his schedule. "Can you pick me up at the airport next Friday?"

"The third?"

"The tenth."

"Sure." But there was a trace of disappointment in Noah's voice.

Cameron rolled the returning tension out of his shoulders and neck. It wasn't as if he didn't want to see Noah sooner. Changing the subject might help. "Did the Yankees win today?"

〜〜〜

Noah didn't even wait for Joey to take his seat across from him at the coffee shop. "Cam's taking off next weekend to come down to see me."

"That's nice, hon."

"That's all I get? 'That's nice, hon.'"

Joey showed much too much tongue ring to just sip on a straw. "You haven't listened to a word I've said about him so why should I waste my time?"

"I did listen," Noah protested. "You told me he liked me. That this had a shot."

"And?"

"And that the problem wasn't him it was me." Though Noah couldn't see how. He wasn't the one who kept leaving. He wasn't the one who'd take off screaming at the mention of some kind of relationship.

"And have you done anything to fix that? Have you done anything to make him think that this is something other than the longest teenage crush in history?"

"I—he—" Joey didn't understand. He hadn't woken up alone those times. He hadn't had Cam try to avoid looking at him when they fucked. Noah had gotten them this far doing things his way. He couldn't risk pushing harder.

"You still look at him like you're looking *up* at him," Joey said around another suck on his straw.

"What are you saying, that I don't act like an adult?"

"What I keep saying is that it's exhausting to try to be the ideal, to live up to being the image of someone's perfect guy."

"Yeah. I'd know all about that, wouldn't I?"

Joey set down his cup. He blinked twice and looked away.

Noah wished he could take it back. "Joey, God. I'm sorry."

Joey let out a long, slow sigh. "No. It was fair. Bitchy, but fair." He picked up his iced macchiato again. "But I've learned a few things since then." He leaned in. "I'm going to tell you a secret. And if you tell anyone, I swear I'll tell Mark you tried to make out with me at our last Halloween party."

"But I didn't."

"But I'll still tell him you did. So listen."

Noah pressed forward on the table.

"Even Mark likes to be taken care of once in a while."

Noah's brain provided a bizarre picture. "Are you telling me—what? You fetch his slippers and pipe?"

"Not like that." Joey's looks were always eloquent. This one said *You're such an idiot, Noah.*

Noah's mental image got even more freaky. "*You* top him?"

"No."

"Think beyond sex and clichés. If you can."

Noah shook his head. "How do you mean?"

Joey smiled, and it was so fucking self-satisfied Noah wanted to come up with another bitchy remark just to get that smirk off Joey's lips.

"What works for us isn't going to work for you. But you've got to stop letting—no expecting—Cam to make all the moves in your relationship, or there's never going to be one."

$$\sim\!\!\sim$$

From his seat on Noah's couch, Cameron looked up as Noah came out of his bedroom. Desire hit Cameron like a punch to the gut. "If you really want to make it out to dinner, you might want to change that shirt."

"I thought you liked it."

"I do. That's the problem."

"Then I guess you'll have fun at dinner."

"Noah—" Cameron took a deep breath. He wasn't going to let a stupid blue-striped shirt control his dick. He'd managed to get over his reaction to the sound and smell of pump rooms and could usually get through Yankees games without needing to jerk off. If he saw Noah more often, he wouldn't be able to get to Cameron like this. "As long as I don't have to wear a tie, I'll be fine."

He had no idea why Noah was so determined to haul them out to some restaurant for dinner. Usually when they dragged themselves out of bed, they just got room service or delivery.

Noah's mood had been bouncing between excited and anxious since Cameron had gotten there two hours ago. Noah had even been too distracted for hey-good-to-see-you sex. As soon as Cameron had cleared the door, Noah had pounced on Cameron with dinner plans.

Cameron watched Noah pace. "This isn't some super spicy Indian food place, is it? Because you've got some weird tastes, man."

"I like you."

"Funny."

Noah straddled him, legs filling up the rest of the couch. "I like the way you taste."

Noah's kiss was slow and deep. His tongue curled and pulled Cameron's back into his mouth while those long-fingered hands worked Cameron's shoulders. Cameron would never admit how good that felt after just a two-hour flight. He brought his own hands up to rub at Noah's jaw, smooth and soft from a recent shave. Cameron breathed in the sharp-as-cut-pine scent of Noah's aftershave.

When Cameron's thumbs swept behind Noah's ears, Noah groaned and took the kiss deeper, hips rocking closer. He was so sensitive there. Actually, Cameron had yet to find a spot where Noah wasn't sensitive to touch. The quick heat of Noah's response kept fueling his own gotta-have-you-now desire.

He used the leverage on Noah's jaw to pull him away. "How

serious are you about going out to eat?"

"I made reservations."

"Then you'd better get off me."

Noah swung off with a dimpling grin that really didn't help Cameron's brain concentrate on anything except getting Noah back on the couch minus his pants.

Food. Dinner. Reservation.

"Reservations? And I don't need a tie?" Cameron asked again.

"Nope."

As they pulled up, Cameron could see why dress was informal. The restaurant looked like an old house—a house that had had too much to drink and was leaning heavily to the right onto a couple of scrubby pines which were hardly up to the task. Noah squeezed his truck onto the grass at the back of the packed lot. The food couldn't be too bad if the lot was this full.

The floor of the bar was sticky and, like everything else about the building, had a pronounced tilt. Cameron wondered if this was what it was like on an old sailing ship. The conditions didn't seem to bother the crowd of people. Through the smoke, Cameron smelled something that teased his memory. Someone moved and he got another whiff. He almost spoke the word out loud. *Babci?*

The dining room was marginally quieter and free of smoke. The hostess led them to the one remaining booth. The red vinyl seats appeared to have lost a fight with an angry cougar, but the table was clean. He sank into the sagging bench and took the menu.

The smell was stronger in here. He could have been twelve again, standing in Babci's kitchen as she pulled a pan of golumbki out of the oven. Cameron swallowed hard as he glanced down at his menu. He hoped to God it was dark enough to hide the water in his eyes.

"I remembered how much you liked your grandmother's cooking. They've got lots of different stuff here, but they're famous for their Polish food," Noah said.

Cameron nodded since he didn't trust his voice. He had to get a grip. His eyes focused on the listings for pierogi, kielbasa, kapusta. Babci's funeral was the only time in his adult life when he'd cried.

"It's all right, isn't it?" Noah's anxious question brought Cameron under control. He looked up and dragged a smile to his lips.

"Yeah, it's great. Thanks, Noah. I haven't had Polish food since...in ages."

"Adam hated it, you know. Hated all the cabbage."

"I remember." Cameron nodded again.

"So what are you going to have?"

"Have you been here before?"

Noah shook his head. The hair fell over his eyes, and he brushed it back.

Cameron's fingers twitched with the urge to do it for him. He wanted to pull him across the crooked table and kiss him for finding this place. For remembering. Just for—he swallowed. But now he didn't have to fake his smile. "I think I'm having everything."

"Sure you are. Because I'm buying." Noah grinned.

"Don't worry. I'll be a good date. I'll put out."

Noah's brows arched. "Really?"

"You'll have to wait and see."

"I think I'm ordering you extra beers."

An hour later, Noah pinched the last pierogi from Cameron's plate, but even Noah couldn't finish the chrusciki they ordered. After Cameron's indecision over the dessert menu, Noah ordered a poppy seed streusel cake and kolacky to go. Cameron wondered if he had a pronounced waddle as they made their way out to the truck.

In Noah's apartment Cameron collapsed on the couch and couldn't even look in the bakery boxes. "That was great."

"Look at you. All relaxed without sex or baseball."

"Gimme half an hour."

"For sex or baseball?" Noah switched on the TV as he dropped down next to him.

"Either. Both."

Cameron never made it to the bottom of the first inning. When he opened his eyes, the TV was off. His head had flopped onto Noah's shoulder. As Cameron straightened up, Noah pushed to his feet and reached down to Cameron.

"This couch is really uncomfortable to sleep on, trust me."

Cameron let Noah tug him to his feet.

Noah turned on the lights in the bedroom and as soon as they undressed for bed, Cameron just wasn't that tired anymore.

He pulled Noah down on top of him.

"Man. I was beginning to think I'd wasted all those beers and all that money on dinner." Noah grinned.

Cameron tongued the dimple that had been teasing him all night, flicking along that deep groove in Noah's cheek. He tasted like sugar from the chrusciki.

"Hmmm. While I've got you there..." Noah slid down Cameron's chest with a series of tingling nips until Noah got to Cameron's navel.

"Rest stop?" Cameron lifted his head from the pillow.

"Nope." Noah pulled on Cameron's legs and towed him to the edge of the bed. "I'm just getting comfortable on the floor since I plan to be here awhile."

Cameron had dragged a pillow along with him and now he tucked it under his head. He wouldn't go so far as to say that watching Noah suck him off was as good as the actual blowjob, but it definitely added to the experience.

Noah smiled up at Cameron from his navel before continuing down with soft kisses and quick bites on his lower belly. When Noah tugged hard on the hair with his teeth, Cameron shivered. Noah paused to look up again.

The expression in his eyes made Cameron feel like he was about to be consumed by Noah's ever-present intensity. And Cameron couldn't—didn't want to stop it. He wanted to give Noah everything he wanted to take. Cameron couldn't remember anyone ever looking at him like that, like all he wanted was to taste him, pull him into his mouth. That hunger should have scared Cameron—maybe something about Noah had always scared Cameron—but right now he just wanted to burn up in that need.

Noah's big hands stroked up Cameron's thighs, nails tickling the skin, thumbs rubbing the crease of his groin. Noah's nose was pressing into Cameron's skin as that soft mouth licked and sucked his sac, lips stretching wide. Cameron pushed up on his elbows to watch, then fell back when the pressure got too tight, too much, too good.

Noah released Cameron's balls and kissed up the side of his cock. Those lips were satin and sun-warm, tongue hot as he lapped and slicked Cameron's dick. He leaned up again, wanting to see Noah's face when he took him in. Noah used his hands now, on balls and shaft, and Cameron wondered if he'd go crazy if Noah didn't start sucking soon. Noah brushed the head across his lips, his cheeks. Cameron panted, watching, waiting.

Noah teased. Tongue on the head, just around the rim, flicking hard underneath. Everything but sensation slipped away until all Cameron's brain knew was what was happening between his thighs. Noah opened his mouth and guided Cameron in, over the softness of Noah's palate down into the velvet constriction of his throat. All the while his tongue worked along the pulsing veins, pressing on the tip.

The rush of pleasure dragged Cameron's eyelids down, even as his hips started to roll to match Noah's bobbing motion. Noah groaned as if he were the one with a mouth around his dick, pure delight vibrating back into Cameron from Noah's throat. The fingers on Cameron's sac slipped lower, pressing and stroking more pleasure out of him.

Noah's mouth got incredibly tighter, hotter, wetter, which is probably why Cameron didn't notice until Noah's finger was already sliding into Cameron's ass, buried to the hilt before he could blink. Too smooth and slick to be spit, Noah must have stashed some lube somewhere. Cameron should say something about Noah not getting any big ideas, but everything felt too good to argue about.

Ecstasy kept Cameron lightheaded enough that his protest at the second finger got swallowed on a moan. A moment of clarity let him think for a second about what Noah was doing, how Cameron could feel Noah combing inside, feeling for that swelling against his fingers. There. And that was Cameron's last conscious thought. He gave in and let pleasure use him, push him until everything came back into sharp focus when he hit that release. Heat and pressure pounded him until the motion of his hips stuttered and froze, and he pumped down Noah's throat. Noah stuck with him, riding every last spurt with him, slowing to licks as Cameron went soft.

Those long fingers were a lot more noticeable going out than they had been going in. He noticed a lot now. His hands had a death grip in Noah's hair; his thighs ached almost as much as his throat. God, what had he said—yelled?

Noah's mouth was kissing the inside of Cameron's thigh when he freed his hands, one finger at a time. Noah looked up when Cameron could finally move his head. He licked dry lips. "Uh?"

Noah smiled. "Just a lot of *oh fuck*s. But I'm surprised the neighbors haven't called."

"Oh fuck." Cameron's abs couldn't seem to hold his head up anymore, and he collapsed back onto the bed.

Noah climbed up, cock thick and blood-dark against his belly. Cameron reached for Noah because Cameron wasn't that kind of guy, but Noah pulled out of reach. "Wait a few minutes. I'm so hard I'd shoot too soon to enjoy it anyway."

Cameron tried to figure a way to get them both comfortable on the bed that didn't require using any of his muscles. Noah took care of it, curling up behind. Noah's chest against Cameron's back felt wide enough to land an airplane on, and he pressed back into that hard warmth as Noah's mouth moved across the back of his neck. Cameron should turn, do something for the erection he could feel poking his thigh, but he just needed a few more minutes. Noah slid a hand around Cameron's hips, shifting until that hard dick slid between Cameron's thighs, nudging right up against Cameron's balls.

Noah's mouth started sucking as he rocked back and forth, his hand sliding up and down the length of Cameron's torso before Noah pressed Cameron against the motion of Noah's hips. A harsh gasp tingled Cameron's wet skin as he arched back against Noah. An impossible desire wound through

Cameron.

"Do it."

Noah froze. The tension in his muscles quivered along Cameron's back.

"Go ahead."

Noah still didn't move.

"I thought you said you could make me come. Here's your chance."

Noah rolled away and was back in a breath. Cameron willed his body to relax and waited for Noah to move him onto his stomach or back, but Noah kept Cameron pressed against that broad chest while hooking his leg up and over Noah's own.

Cold lube brushed against him, too cool to be anything but fingers.

"Don't need any more. I can take it."

"I don't want you to take it. I want you to come, remember?"

Just two of Noah's fingers were thicker and longer than some of the cocks Cameron had had in his mouth. Noah's leg kept Cameron open but, being on his side like this, all he had to do to stop that slow twisting stretch was to roll away.

He liked this. He wasn't too sure how he was going to feel about it when those scissoring fingers turned into Noah's dick, but this was a lot better than he remembered. Noah's fingers pressed and circled super-sensitive nerves.

Cameron's dick came back to life with a painful rush of blood. Noah's fingers fucked into him now, quick thrusts that made Cameron want to press back to keep them trapped deep inside. He opened his eyes. Noah was watching, mouth open and wet on the top of Cameron's shoulder.

The flood of embarrassment was as powerful as his

arousal. He couldn't imagine how ridiculous he looked, what kind of face he made as he rode Noah's fingers.

"Cam. Feel so good. So smooth and tight and hot." Noah's words twisted inside along with his fingers, pumping more heat to his cock.

"C'mon then," Cameron gasped.

"Now who's pushy?"

"Shut up," was all Cameron could say, because fuck *you* was entirely inappropriate to the situation.

He'd heard often enough that the first inch was the hardest, that strain of coaxing the muscles to open, but it still took his breath away.

Noah leaned down and kissed him through it. Cameron thought a hand on his dick would probably be more helpful. He let out a long breath, and his nerves stayed on the good side of pain as Noah slid deeper.

"Move."

Noah jerked his hips in short, tight strokes, just enough to tease rolling bursts of sweetness from inside him.

Cameron turned to watch Noah's face, to watch him bite his lower lip as he quickened the pace. Cameron reached back to grab his own calf to keep himself steady.

Noah slowed again, his hair tickling Cameron's cheek as Noah leaned in to kiss him. His hand finally found its way to Cameron's ready cock.

"Yeah," he murmured against Noah's lips. Cameron's body agreed, shuddering as the speed of Noah's hips increased to match the stroke on Cameron's dick. "Faster. Harder. God—"

His belly lurched as he yielded to the power of that explosion building up inside, let it fill his veins with liquid nitrogen and burn him from the inside out.

Noah was everywhere, around Cameron, in him—mouth, cock, hand, body. Noah's almost-there grunts reverberated against Cameron's back even as they tickled his ear.

"Harder," he said again. *Don't, Noah, please hang on.*

Then as Noah slammed forward, Cameron realized he'd only had half of Noah's cock. The shock of being so full so fast flung Cameron like a slingshot. He jerked into Noah's fist in time with the sound of *Cam* in his ear. Noah kissed Cameron back into his body, hand shifting up to grab Cameron's thigh as Noah stuttered through his own release.

Noah slumped, folded around Cameron, heart thudding against his back. It was good. God, he sounded stupid, but it felt...safe, right. He didn't think he'd want to be on this side of things often, but it hadn't been like those other times.

Noah's breath huffed in his ear.

Cameron opened his eyes in alarm. "You're not going to fall asleep in me?"

"No." Noah's laugh rumbled into his back.

"Good."

Noah took a few more breaths and rolled away. When he came back, his big body was welcome heat in spots that had gone cold. As Noah tugged Cameron back against that chest, he mumbled, "You do realize that I'm going to be fucking you through the mattress in a few hours."

"Absolutely," Noah agreed.

〰〰〰

Noah woke in a panic. Cam hadn't backed up that sleepy promise, and Noah was half-afraid he'd find Cam gone. He reached out and found Cam's hip.

Thank God, Noah hadn't pushed Cam too far. Maybe there was something in what Joey had been trying to say. If nothing else came of it, Noah had a whole new collection of jerk-off fantasies and wet dreams to entertain him until the next time Cam came to see him. Because there was always a next time. Noah couldn't think about there not being a next time.

Cam shifted and flung out an arm. Noah looked over. Somehow the bastard had swiped his pillow. Since Cam only had one, he'd probably stolen Noah's to replace his own after Cam had thrown it on the floor. Noah had to remember to buy an extra one for when Cam stayed. Cam was too used to sleeping alone in a hotel's king-sized bed with three pillows. What they really needed was a California king with lots of pillows and a solid iron headboard they could both hang onto for extra leverage.

Oh shit. His previous fantasies involving Cameron had never gotten as far as buying furniture together. That would, of course, mean they were living together. Which was never going to happen since as near as Noah could figure Cam lived in hotels, and Noah had a job he loved in Tallahassee.

He squeezed his eyes shut as if he could push the image of their bed from his brain. Green sheets to match Cam's eyes? No. No bed.

"That is the worst fake sleep I've ever seen."

Noah opened his eyes to see Cam facing him, head on his stolen pillow, eyes dark green in the sun streaming through the curtain.

"I wasn't faking, I was—" *picturing us living together.*

"I don't know, Noah. I thought you were supposed to be good at this. You fuck a guy, don't offer him a towel to clean up, and then you fake sleep so you don't have to get up and get him coffee?"

Noah would have decked Cam with a pillow, but he had them all.

Cam sighed. "Fine. I'll get the coffee. You know I can't say no to you."

You haven't seemed to have any trouble with that so far. But then again, Noah hadn't really asked Cam for what he wanted. The truth was Noah couldn't say no to Cam. Ever. *Noah, cut off your dick and hand it to me. Here you go, Cam.*

"Where should I go?"

"Uh—to my coffeemaker? You do know how to use one? It's a machine they sometimes have in hotel rooms where there's no room service."

Cameron threw his own pillow at Noah and bounced to the edge of the bed. "Damn." He sounded surprised.

Noah sat up. God, had he hurt Cam last night?

"I forgot all about the kolacky. I'd have been eating breakfast hours ago."

Noah watched Cam's ass as he headed for the kitchen. Smiling, Noah leaned over and collected the pillows from the floor.

Cam came back in a few minutes with two mugs and a bakery box. "This is how you plan to spend the day? Naked in bed? I approve." He sat down, appropriated both pillows and handed off one mug while he opened the bakery box. "See, this is how you treat a guy you've fucked. Cookies and coffee in bed."

"Really? Because I thought the thing to do was to disappear while he was sleeping."

Cam sent up a cloud of powdered sugar as he dropped his kolacky back in the box. "Fucking hell, Noah. That was seven years ago."

Noah knew that. He did. And he suspected that even his nineteen-year-old self would have had better self-control than to blurt that out.

Cam shoved the box off his lap. "Is that what all this has been about? It's weird payback for something that happened seven fucking years ago?"

"No." It might have been—just at first—but no. Now it was about green sheets and kolacky in bed. But trying to explain all that wouldn't help now.

Cam pulled his clothes off the top of the dresser. "You know what? I'm going out. For a paper or something. And just so you know, I am coming the fuck back. See if you can grow up a little in the next twenty minutes."

Cam was more than twenty minutes, but then Noah supposed Cam needed the extra time. Noah knew he did. Maybe it was a small sign of maturity that he didn't punch anything, though the tiles in the shower were seriously tempting him. But he wasn't even angry. Not at Cam—or the tiles. He wasn't even sure if he was angry at himself, though he knew he definitely should be.

Did he still resent Cam for leaving that night? Maybe a little. But so much had happened since Noah had seen Cam again. They weren't even the same guys, really. And if Noah was ready to start thinking about...beds, he should have gotten over it.

He was reaching for a towel when he heard Cam come back in. The stereo flipped on. Noah couldn't hide in the bathroom forever. If this was a fight with Joey, Noah would know what to do. He'd apologize, and Joey would bust out with his therapy crap and they'd figure out what they were both actually pissed about. It had been one of the worst and best things about living with a social worker.

But Joey wasn't waiting out there. Cam was. Noah still needed to apologize, at least for ruining breakfast.

He pulled on a pair of shorts and ran a comb through his wet hair.

True to his word, Cam had brought back a newspaper. There was a familiar beige cup in his hand, so he'd also found his way to Grounds for Improvement.

Noah took a deep breath. "Sorry."

Cam looked up.

"I was being a jerk, I'm sorry."

It was as if Cam were waiting for something else, but Noah didn't know what else Cam expected Noah to say.

Cam folded the paper and tossed it on the coffee table. "It's okay."

But Noah knew it wasn't. "You want to go down to the beach? Carrabelle's really nice."

Cam picked up the paper again. "You know what I never get to do? Go to the movies. The new Spiderman movie is playing at the Imax theater."

Considering the awkward strain between them, maybe an hour in the car, plus beach traffic and ninety-five degree heat would be a bad idea. A movie—well at least then Noah wouldn't be able to say anything else stupid.

"Sounds good."

They each bought their own ticket. The action sequences were amazing on the giant screen, just not enough to distract Noah from the tension running barbed wire through his neck and shoulders.

Chapter Seven

On the way home, they stopped at Georgie's to pick up subs. Noah was glad he had to concentrate on driving, because he still couldn't figure out how to fix the silence dragging between them.

This was stupid. Tomorrow Cam was leaving again, and they hadn't even talked about when Cam would be back. If Noah was going to screw this up, he was going down fighting.

Noah stowed the subs in the fridge. Cam was still standing by the door, looking as if the only reason he wasn't leaving was because he'd prove Noah right. Noah grabbed him around the waist. Cam didn't resist, but he didn't respond either.

"I'm such an asshole. I don't know why I said that," Noah offered.

"Yeah, well, maybe that's something you should figure out."

What did Cam expect him to say? It was goddamned obvious that it had hurt.

Noah swallowed. "Could have left a note."

Cam pushed away. "What did you think, Noah? We were going to go down to the wedding brunch holding hands and tell everyone we'd be registered at Sur La Table, thanks very much?"

"Do you have to be such a fucking bastard about everything?"

"Only when you're being such a brat." Cam's hand rasped across his cheeks as he scrubbed at his face. "You know, I really have to wonder. If I pissed you off that much, what the hell made you so quick to jump back in bed with me?"

"Because I never stopped wanting you." *Oh. Fuck.* That was the second time today Noah's mouth had gotten him into serious trouble and he had nothing like a few shots of tequila or a dick up his ass to blame the lack of control on. "And now—"

"Now what?" Cam stepped back toward him.

Noah's throat squeezed shut. Now he couldn't get the words out? Now he couldn't explain that he was terrified he'd just fucked up everything and he wanted to go back to bed and start this whole shitastic day over again?

Cam gave a tiny shake of his head and reached up to cup the back of Noah's neck. As Cam pulled him closer, Noah felt the kick in his lower belly like someone had turned on the acid pump. He wasn't sure what kind of kiss to expect, but he'd never have expected Cam to flat out seduce him with his mouth. To kiss him until all Noah could think of was how good that mouth felt on his dick, his ass, his neck. Cam kissed him like he was promising the best oral sex in the universe, and Noah's body remembered that Cam could deliver.

Cam dragged Noah closer with an arm around his waist, held him steady under the licking, sucking, fucking of his mouth. Noah clung to Cam's shoulders and hung on as his body moved into Cam's like Noah was trying to shift all of his atoms about six inches over. He wanted their clothes gone, wanted their bodies to fit inside each other in perfect spontaneity. A groan of frustration burned his throat.

His back hit the wall as Cam shoved him forward and then

their hips aligned, cocks rubbing side by side, trapped under their shorts. Noah was going to fucking come in his pants, from nothing more than Cam kissing him like that—pure sex in every lick of his tongue, every suck on Noah's lips.

Cam's hand found the belt holding Noah's shorts on his hips and unhooked it with one hand. Noah got his own hands between them. But with the way his hands were shaking, he wasn't much help with the button or the zipper. Cam pushed Noah's hands out of the way and then his shorts were gone. Cam pulled Noah's cock through the slit in his briefs while Noah's fingers—even less coordinated with Cam's hand stroking his dick—worked at Cam's shorts.

Cam lifting off Noah's mouth was almost as devastating as Cam's lips pulling off Noah's cock. Moving him out of the way again, Cam freed his own dick. He wrapped his hand around the base of them both so that their cocks slid against each other in Cam's fist.

"No. Wanna fuck," Noah demanded.

"Let me drive, okay?" Cam had never asked him before. Just told him. The last bit of apprehension evaporated in the heat pumping through him.

"Yeah."

Cam took his mouth again as his hips and hand worked them together. The friction was almost too rough and dry, already stretched-taut skin tugged tighter. Cam's thumb found the drops of precome and spread them down, and the friction got better.

Noah wasn't usually this quick on the draw, but if Cam didn't stop Noah was going to shoot faster than he had since he was fourteen. Cam kept kissing him, so Noah couldn't tell Cam about it, not that Noah would anyway since he'd already screwed up enough running his mouth. He dug his hands hard into Cam's collarbone and thrust back into that tight fist so his dick slid opposite Cam's.

It was right there, warning sparks arcing to his balls. And Cam stopped, only held their cocks pressed together, no friction, just pressure, and Noah's body snatched back that promised pleasure so fast it recoiled up his spine like a spring.

"Goddamn it," he panted. "You..."

"Fucking bastard?" Cam suggested with an arch of his brow.

Noah sighed.

Cam smiled. "It's gonna feel even better when you let it go."

Noah barely realized they were moving through the room before Cam stopped.

"How sturdy is your coffee table?"

Noah had cut it down from an old butcher block table he'd found at a yard sale, leaving the legs long enough to be a bit taller than the sofa's seat. "Guess we'll find out." He stripped off his shirt, and then the difficulty of extracting himself from his briefs made him reconsider the boxer option—or at least the wisdom of leaving briefs on when receiving a Cameron Lewis hand job.

Cam gave him a nudge. Noah dropped to his knees.

"Lay out on it for me."

Noah seemed to have forgotten how to control his body unless Cam told him what to do.

"God, Noah, you look—" Cam crowded in behind, heat shivering down skin that had been sweat cooled. He kissed the back of Noah's neck, the line of his shoulder blade before running a pointed tongue down Noah's spine.

A pulse of anticipation tightened the muscles of his ass, but as soon as Cam got to the base of Noah's spine, Cam stopped and licked a circle around Noah's tailbone. He gripped the legs of the coffee table and rolled his body to get closer to Cam's mouth.

"So good, so hot," Cam murmured.

Cam made another sweep down Noah's back, tongue and fingers electrifying the skin. Noah's dick must have weighed about forty pounds by now, so thick and heavy it pulled at his groin, strained the muscles in his lower back and thighs. The chill of the varnish had felt good when he first stretched out, but now the table only trapped his cock against his belly with the kind of pressure that only made the ache worse.

As Cam ran his thumbs up the crease and pulled Noah's ass open, he ground his forehead against the maple boards. His diaphragm had shifted halfway up into his throat, making his breath fast and shallow. That was why the sound he made when Cam's tongue circled his hole was so high and thin. Cam licked Noah, teased him, got him slippery enough with spit that Cam's finger slid in smooth and deep, flicking the edge of that knot of pleasure inside.

Noah had time for a brief regret as Cam withdrew his finger and used his thumbs to press Noah wide open again. He should have done this to Cam last night when he had the chance. Then Cam was fucking Noah with his tongue, hot and slick, and *sweet Jesus* groaning against him and Noah couldn't think anymore. Could barely breathe. Wood creaked in protest under his fingers, but he didn't care if he ripped the legs off the damn table because he had to hold on. Cam's thumbs slid in next to his tongue. Heat poured down Noah's thighs until the muscles trembled and melted. He hung there, panting, while Cam stretched Noah with thumbs and mouth before moving to suck a deep bite into the top of Noah's ass.

Cam ran both hands up the muscles of Noah's back.

Without the distraction of Cam's mouth and fingers, Noah's dick reminded him how much he needed to come.

"Stop teasing," he groaned.

Cam leaned over Noah's back to growl in his ear. "It's only teasing if I'm not going to do it. And you, babe, are definitely getting fucked." He peeled away. "Gotta get the lube."

"Don't need it." Noah was slick enough.

"Need to get a condom anyway."

There was that. Noah turned his head on the hard planks while he listened to his breathing slow. Cam appeared in the hallway. Watching had almost the same effect Cam rimming him had. Noah's skin buzzed, his bones melted and he couldn't think about anything but having Cam inside. Now.

"So you don't need lube?" Cam was behind him again.

Noah thought about how rash that might have been.

Cam laid his body over Noah and held his arms. "What do you want, Noah?" There was no teasing growl in his voice, only a hoarse demand.

"You." It took two breaths with Cam's weight on him and something else pinning Noah's tongue to the roof of his mouth but he got it out. "Fuck me."

"Listen to me. If I do you without lube, it's gonna hurt. You want that? Is that what you need?"

"No." But Noah could hear the hesitation in his own voice. The question. That had been the last straw with Joey. Joey hadn't just wanted a top he'd wanted a Dom. Noah couldn't give Joey that. Was this why?

"We'll see about that when your head's on straight. I got what you need now, babe."

Even with the lube it was almost too much at first. Six weeks was a long time between fucks with Cam as a lover. He

131

didn't give Noah time to catch his breath but pulled his hips up higher and fucked him. Noah started to reach for his cock, needing something to counter the overwhelming sensation of Cam pounding deep inside.

"No. Hold onto the table."

There was no reason why Noah should. Except that he did. Because Cam told him to.

And just like that his brain and body relaxed, gave in and let Cam take over.

Cam did. Fast and good, rubbing right across Noah's prostate until the lightest pressure on his dick would have sent him over, and then Cam would stop, slow to a grind. A swiveling hard pressure that made Noah tighten his fingers around the table legs to keep from grabbing his dick. Cam moved Noah wherever Cam wanted him with hands at Noah's hips, holding him steady for long strokes, the head of Cam's thick cock catching, stretching the rim before he sank in so far Noah could feel Cam all the way up to his throat.

"That's it, babe."

Cam went deep and ground into Noah again, a swivel of hips that put Noah right on the knife-edge of pleasure and pain until he thought maybe his eyeballs would turn themselves inside out.

He had his teeth clenched, but the word slipped out anyway. "Please."

"What do you want? Gotta tell me."

"I have to come." Noah was a fraction of a second away from begging, pleading. The broken refrain of *please, please, please* rolled through his head one breath away from spilling out of his throat.

"I know. When I tell you."

Cam lifted Noah, until just his shoulders were on the table, and snapped into him until it was nothing but a blur of friction he could feel in every nerve in his body.

"Now. Come," Cam urged.

Noah had to prop himself up with one hand, but when he finally-God-finally got his hand on his cock it was worth it. He came harder and longer than he ever had in his life. Came so long he thought he'd damage something if he didn't stop. And he never wanted it to stop. His body was still shaking so hard he wasn't sure he had stopped when Cam pulled him onto the floor.

Cam kissed his neck, his shoulder, behind his ear, his breath still sharp and loud. Noah felt him soft and wet against his thigh so he knew Cam had come, Noah just wished he'd been able to pay attention to it while it was happening.

He rubbed his head against Cam's biceps to get the sweat-stuck hair out of his eyes. "Have you done that before?"

"Yeah. Some. I wouldn't want to do it all the time. Gets a little intense."

Noah leaned back against Cam's chest. "I noticed."

Cam laughed softly in Noah's ear and kissed him again. "Guess so."

〰〰

Something about having Cam around always seemed to drag Noah out of sleep far too early. It was barely light out when his eyes popped open. Cam wasn't there. But Noah knew he hadn't left. Somehow yesterday had cured him of the idea that Cam would disappear if he closed his eyes too long.

He found Cam in the living room, his laptop open on the

coffee table. *The coffee table, Jesus.*

Cam looked up at him and winked. Warmth spilled out from Noah's stomach. He wanted to wake up to that wink every morning. Just then, their bed with the green sheets and an iron frame didn't seem so far away.

"Don't you ever sleep?"

"You sleep enough for the both of us. We went to bed at eight o'clock."

"Someone wore me out." Noah pushed the hair out of his eyes.

Cam smiled.

"What's so important you had to see it at five fucking o'clock in the morning?" Noah asked.

"Got plans for Labor Day weekend?"

Noah yawned and thought about it. "Not that I can think of."

"I'll be in Orlando. Want to meet me?"

♒

Cameron picked the phone up and put it down again. This was a pretty big deal. He'd been thinking about it since June. He should have decided sooner, given Noah a little more time.

He thought about it again and picked up the phone.

Five rings. Maybe—

"Hey."

—he should have done this face-to-face.

"Do you think you could get the second week of November off?" Cameron asked.

"I don't know. Why?" Noah's voice sounded softer than usual.

"Well, Havers has a big conference every other year."

"Yeah."

"And it's in Hawaii." Cameron waited a second for Noah to connect the dots.

"Hawaii?" The excitement was there, but dampened with a big wet dose of doubt.

"If you can get the time, I want you to come with me."

Cameron could swing it. Picking up the extra cost on the room to bring a guest—which most of the attendees did anyway—wouldn't be a problem. Noah's plane ticket would wipe out his reward miles, but he'd earn them back in two years with all the flying he did.

"I'd love to, but—"

"But you just don't like beautiful tropical beaches."

"I can't afford it." Noah sounded like he really wished he could.

"The hotel's paid for."

"I know, but the ticket."

"I'll handle the ticket," Cameron said.

"No."

"Just no?" That wasn't a word he heard out of Noah often.

"Look. I'll see about the time and I'll see if I can afford a ticket."

Cameron knew Noah couldn't. The ticket would be at least a grand. Maybe more. "It won't cost me anything. You know I've got so many frequent flyer miles I could book a spot on the next space shuttle."

"No," Noah repeated.

Cameron remembered the conference two years ago. The gay beach, the bar, all those gorgeous guys. But he didn't want a random piece of ass to fuck. He wanted Noah. Cameron wanted Noah to talk to on the long plane ride. He wanted Noah to hit the beach with.

"Hawaii, babe."

"I'll see. I'll call you back tomorrow." Maybe Noah was afraid Cameron would change his mind if they kept talking.

"Wait."

"What?"

"How's your right hand?"

"Getting pretty tired." Even Noah's voice had dimples.

"What about the left?"

"On the verge of carpal tunnel. Think your bosses would give me workman's comp for repetitive motion injury?"

"You think if you got both hands working together...?"

"I'm going to need a better line than that."

"Got one." Cameron tucked the phone under his ear. "You think if you put both of them on that hot cock of yours I could listen to you jerk off?"

"What, no pay-per-view porn?"

"Not tonight." Cameron heard clothes rustling, closed his eyes and pictured Noah popping his fly, pulling his cock through—no. "Take them all the way off."

Noah's breath hitched. "Okay."

That last sex. Oh yeah. Cameron knew he had a dominant streak, but Noah brought it out in Cameron like nobody else. When Noah looked at Cameron like he could do anything to him and Noah would keep coming back for more, Cameron had to give Noah exactly what he was begging for. Noah yielding, knuckles going white as he clung to the legs of the table, doing everything Cameron told him—after that, Cameron had come like his fucking life depended on it. His hand started to stroke slow and sure on his cock.

"What have you been thinking about that's got your hand so tired?"

Noah groaned.

"Me fucking you?" Cameron asked.

"Sometimes it's me fucking *you*."

Cameron's hips bucked and his fist tightened. Because that was part of what made Noah's submission so goddamned sweet. That Noah had fucked him the night before, and Cameron had liked it. And Noah still let Cameron push him as far as he had. "Yeah?"

"Definitely." Noah's breath panted in his ear. "Loved fucking you. What do you think about?"

Your face when you come. The taste of you in my mouth. "The way your ass feels around my cock." *That, too.* "The way you slam back against me when I fuck you deep."

Noah gave one of those whimpers.

Precome leaked from his slit, and Cameron thumbed it over and down, slicking the twist of his fingers under the crown. He should have grabbed the lube before he dialed.

"Next week, babe. Gonna fuck you in every position I can think of and some I'm going to have to look up."

"Oh yeah." Noah's groans were getting deeper, harsher, an occasional whimper that Cameron just knew was Noah's thumb pressing hard on the head.

Cameron worked his hand faster. "Gonna fuck the taste right out of your mouth."

Noah's response was nothing but a long moan.

"You got lube with you, babe?"

"Uhhhn."

"You know what I want you to do. Let me hear it." The image of Noah fingering himself, those long fingers disappearing into his ass, burned behind Cameron's lids. Cameron choked off a moan to listen.

"Cam."

That was the sound he was waiting for. The pleading hoarse stretch over his name.

"Yeah. Come for me, babe." Cameron jacked himself hard and fast as Noah's sharp cries hit him across all those miles, sizzled down his nerves until it boiled over and out of him on a long muffled moan.

"Noah. Man. You are coming to Hawaii with me. I can't afford the roaming charges."

Noah's laugh in his ear was his only answer.

〜〜〜

Cameron shifted his hips and watched Noah's face. His mouth dropped open at the same time the tension left his thighs. Cameron grabbed onto Noah's hips to keep him there and pumped forward, watching the way each stroke affected Noah's expression. Cameron knew when he hit the right spots inside, knew when he was in to the limit, knew what made Noah sigh and what made him fight for breath.

Noah's hands wrapped around Cameron's wrists and held on.

Cameron closed his eyes and flexed his hips faster. Noah had only been in the Orlando hotel room for two hours and this was the second time they'd fucked. It should have been impossible, but Cameron swore Noah was tighter and hotter around him the second time. Cameron had never wanted more to feel that heat and pressure without the barrier over his skin. He'd never done it. Guys had offered, but he'd always figured anyone who'd risk it was a risk to him. But Noah, Cameron could trust. He usually got tested in December when he had his annual physical, but if he went in next time he was home, and Noah did...and then in six months.

Cameron wanted it. God, how he wanted Noah around him, nothing between them, like when Noah's throat pressed thick and wet as he swallowed around Cameron's cock. He groaned and arched his back, going deep enough to get a desperate sound from Noah.

Cameron opened his eyes. Noah was watching him, mouth slack, chest shining with sweat. He licked his lips. "Where'd you go?"

"Nowhere." Cameron bent down for a kiss, swallowing the sounds Noah made when Cameron rolled his hips in tight circles.

"Good." Noah reached into Cameron's hair and kept him against his mouth, kissed him as hard as the grind of their hips.

Even under the blast from the air conditioner, they were sticky with sweat and come when they pulled apart, but Cameron still hugged Noah close when he came back from flushing the condom. There was a step he was looking forward to eliminating.

Noah was drifting, so Cameron kissed him awake. Noah lifted his head and smiled. "Again?"

"Maybe in little bit. Think you can still deep throat if I'm sucking you off?" They hadn't tried sixty-nining yet. There was a lot they hadn't done yet.

"We'll see."

Cameron tried to find a way to bring up what he wanted. If Noah wasn't ready, Cameron wouldn't push it. He kissed Noah again and smoothed the hair off his forehead. "I haven't been with anyone else since the last time we were together."

Noah tensed and pushed away. That wasn't quite what Cameron had been hoping for.

Neither was the sarcasm that came pouring out of Noah's mouth.

"Gee. That's great. Maybe you could get it printed on a T-shirt. 'Last week I didn't fuck ten random guys.'"

"What the fuck, Noah?"

Noah rolled until he was at the edge of the bed with his back to Cameron.

"Did I miss a conversation? The one where we decided not to fuck around?" Cameron swallowed back the anger that made him just want to vault out of the bed.

Noah dropped onto his back and looked over.

Cameron tightened his jaw. He was not giving into that kicked-puppy look again.

"Or is this just another way of trying to make me feel like a fucking bastard?"

"No." Noah shut his eyes.

Cameron tried to hang on to his temper. "So then maybe you could tell me what gives you the right to say something like that?"

Noah looked at Cameron again. "I haven't been with anyone else since...since I saw you in March."

"Well, why the fuck didn't you say something? How the hell was I going to know?"

Noah raked a hand through his hair and flopped back onto the bed. "I didn't want you to feel like you couldn't."

"So you're pissed because I did?"

Noah's hand reached for his hair again and then he looked at it and pulled it down. "I guess I am." His voice held a trace of amusement. "Pretty stupid of me."

Brat. Cameron wasn't going to let Noah give in and look cute and wiggle out of this one. Cameron wanted to sit on him until he got some answers. He knelt on the bed, knees touching Noah's ribs.

"Why?"

"Why what?"

"Fight like a grownup, Noah. Why are you pissed that I've been with other guys when you never asked me not to?"

Noah came up off his back and leaned right over him, and damn, Cameron had forgotten how big he was.

"Because I'm jealous. All right? I don't want to know about all the random asses you've fucked. And just where do you get off telling me to grow up when your whole life is like an endless fucking vacation?"

"It's not a fucking vacation. It's my job. And I worked damned hard to get it." Cameron sank back on his heels. "You're jealous?"

Noah sighed and his bangs fluttered.

Noah was jealous. That shouldn't be making Cameron want to smile.

Would he be jealous if Noah said he was screwing his cute little ex again? Cameron didn't think so. What if it was that other guy at the party? The one as big as Noah with the dark beard. If those tattooed arms bent Noah over the deck railing—Cameron's hands clenched into fists. Yeah, that would piss him off.

"So why didn't you tell me before?"

"I didn't want to make you feel like you had to do something you didn't want to do."

Cameron could get that. He didn't like being forced into anything. "Okay. I didn't bring it up to hurt you. I was actually trying to say that I wanted to know if we could make this exclusive."

"Why?"

"What do you mean why?"

"You get to ask why and I don't?"

"I don't want to fuck anyone but you." He pulled Noah down onto the bed next to him. The room had gotten cold, cold and damp with the humidity soaking the window like rain.

Noah tangled their legs together, hard muscle and warm skin. Cameron pushed his feet against Noah's, enjoying the stretch in his ankles.

"Why didn't you?" Cameron asked. "I mean, why haven't you been with other guys?"

Noah tensed. It couldn't be for lack of opportunity. Cameron had seen the way some of the guys at that party were looking at Noah.

"Noah?" Maybe Noah had lied about it. Maybe he had been with other guys. But why would he lie? He had no reason to.

"Can we not talk about this?"

Normally, Cameron would say yeah, but he'd just asked Noah to take a pretty big step with him and this evasiveness was bugging him. "No."

Noah rolled away.

Scratch bugging him—insert pissing Cameron the fuck off.

Noah got off the bed and went over to the window, staring out as if there was some kind of answer in those fat drops of water shining silver on the black glass.

"What's going on?" Cameron demanded.

Noah's head tipped back on his neck, but Cameron still couldn't see Noah's face. Cameron wasn't angry anymore, he was worried. The tension in the air made him think Noah was about to confess to having some terminal disease.

"Don't you know? Jesus, I've made such an ass of myself I thought it was obvious." Noah's voice was strained.

Cameron padded over to him, senses so aware he was conscious of each nub in the burgundy carpet even through toughened soles of his feet. The air conditioning roared until it competed with the planes taking off and landing a mile away. Noah's skin sent a chill up Cameron's arm as he put his hand on Noah's shoulder.

"C'mon, Noah." Cameron turned Noah around.

He shut his eyes and swallowed. "I love you."

"Oh."

Chapter Eight

Cameron wasn't proud of his first thought. *Of course you do, I'm taking you to Hawaii.* Hard on the heels of that came, *No you don't. It's just a crush.* He knew what his response was supposed to be though, and it wasn't either of those things or his stammered *oh.* For once in his life, he wasn't ready with the response everyone wanted to hear. He couldn't. It was the right response, *I love you, too,* and he did—but not the way he knew Noah meant it.

Noah was watching his face. And Cameron still hadn't worked out anything to say but that *oh.*

Noah stepped back with a shaky laugh. "Yeah. I really need some clothes."

"I like you naked."

"I don't like me this naked." Noah grabbed the T-shirt Cameron had tossed about thirty seconds after Noah got to the room.

"Noah."

"You keep saying that. Look, can we forget I said that?"

"Forget you said you loved me?"

"Fuck, Cam, are you laughing at me?" Noah found his shorts on the far side of the bed. He had to bend over to get them and the sight of that ass did what it always did to

Cameron.

"No. I'm not laughing." He crossed the room and grabbed Noah's arm before he could pull on those ratty denim shorts. "I'm—" What? Cameron really didn't know. But he wasn't angry or worried or any of those things he'd been a few minutes ago. "I'm happy."

"Happy?" Noah held his shorts and shirt in front of his crotch.

"I shouldn't be happy? A gorgeous guy just said he was in love with me."

"I didn't say that."

Cameron stared Noah down until a dark red spread across his cheeks under his tan. Noah shook his arm free and tried to get a foot in his shorts.

"If you put those on, we'll just have to take them off. And you know how pushy and impatient you get."

"How impatient I get?" Noah held up the shorts. The button was hanging by a thread.

"Should have dropped them when I opened the door."

"You're happy?" Noah let him take the shorts out of his hands and throw them across the room.

"Is that a bad thing?"

"No."

Cameron wished he had something else to give Noah, but Cameron wasn't completely sure being in love wasn't just something people got confused with awesome sex. "C'mon back to bed. It's freezing, and I'm tired of chasing you around the room."

"So turn down the air conditioning."

"You're not coming to bed?"

Noah looked at him. Cameron felt like he'd not only kicked the puppy but stolen all its toys.

He sat on the edge of the bed. "Happy's all I got right now. Gimme a few and I can upgrade it to happy and horny." He leaned back on his hands and looked up. Noah was standing there, still holding his shirt like a lifeline. "Noah. You're the only guy I want in my bed. Is that going to be okay?"

Noah nodded and tossed the shirt after the shorts.

〰〰

Noah thought it was more than okay when Cam woke Noah with a mouth bobbing on his cock. He'd been so tired after the drive down and that conversation, he barely came awake before he pumped his load down Cam's throat. It might have been a pity blowjob, but that didn't make Cam's mouth any less hot or wet.

He lay back with an arm across his eyes and spent about five seconds trying to convince himself that the conversation was a dream, but it didn't work.

It could be worse.

He'd spilled the secret he didn't think was one, and Cam hadn't taken off. Cam hadn't dropped to his knees with declarations of his undying love, but then Noah hadn't been counting on that. Maybe later Cam would freak out, but at the moment he was kissing the inside of Noah's thighs, stubble a teasing scrape as Cameron shifted his head. Was he fucking nuzzling him? Because that wasn't like Cam. And it made it feel much more like pity sex.

Cam licked his way up until he rested his chin on Noah's breastbone. Since he was a little afraid of what he'd see in

Cam's eyes, Noah still had his arm across his face.

"Good morning." Cam's breath hit his neck.

Noah rolled his head to the side under his arm and peeked at the clock. "Morning? It's five thirty. That's almost the middle of the night."

"I'm going to go down to the gym and work out."

Noah thought that was going to make the room pretty empty. "Aren't you hard?"

Cam shifted so that his erection rubbed against Noah's thigh. "But I'm sure you'd rather sleep."

Noah finally pulled his arm down. It was too dark in the room to see much, but Cam's face didn't look like he was anything but horny.

"Climb up here and get in my mouth. I'll show you how sleepy I am."

Cam smiled and shook his head as he straddled Noah's hips and sat on him.

Noah tensed his muscles, testing. He wasn't sore. "Okay."

Cam shook his head again. "I've got other plans."

"Plans?"

Cam's teeth flashed in the dark as he smiled. "Don't strain yourself, Noah. I know you can't function at this hour."

Cam was rocking on him, one hand pressing his cock down on Noah's belly. Cam moved up and down and side to side, painting precome over Noah's abs and chest. Cam's eyes closed and his tongue swept his lips before those teeth sucked his lower lip in. His other hand worked his shaft as he slid that slick head over the ridges in Noah's abs.

Noah licked his own lips in anticipation. "Bring it up here."

Cam opened his eyes. "You need your rest." He brought his

hand up to his mouth and lapped at his fingers and palm.

"God, don't you get enough of your own hand?"

"Not with you like this. Under me. Sucked dry. God, your skin is so hot."

Noah's hands grabbed Cam's hips, and Cam jacked himself faster. He arched forward, lips parting on a soft moan.

"Already?"

"I was jerking off while I blew you, babe."

If Cam had left anything in him, Noah would've been hard again at the thought. But then the sound of Cam's hand on his dick, the smell of sex soaking the air around them made Noah's dick hot and cold and tingly, like a foot coming back from pins and needles but without the pain.

Noah ran his hands up Cam's back, fingers working the muscles hard. Cam moaned again, and his eyes opened. Still heavy lidded, no color in the faint light, expression soft. Happy, just like he'd said.

Cam's lips curved. "Really?"

Noah wished he didn't know what Cam was talking about. "Yes, really."

"Say it again." Cam rubbed his cock all over Noah's belly again, slapped it into his navel.

"No."

"C'mon."

"You're going to get off on it?"

"Yeah." Cam spoke as if there was no doubt about it. Like it would be stupid not to.

Cam really wasn't freaked. And he had to feel something back. Why else would he want to stop screwing around?

Cam's hand was a blur on his dick now. Noah cupped

Cam's balls.

"Noah. Please."

"I love you."

Cam's eyes squeezed shut, and he started those guttural gasps he made just before he came. He really did get off on it. Noah watched the first spurt fly out to land up on his neck. Another gasp and Cam sprayed his pecs with thick warm drops. Noah linked his hand with Cam's as he shuddered through the last spasms. Cam leaned down and kissed him, their chests sliding together on sweat and come.

"Go back to sleep, babe. I'll wake you for breakfast." Cam's tongue licked slow and soft into Noah's mouth.

The buzz of arousal was still there under his skin, riding his bloodstream. He didn't want Cam to leave. "Not that sleepy."

"Then why are you almost asleep?"

"I'm not." But Noah yawned.

"I'll be back in an hour."

〰️〰️

"What do you have to do today?" Noah shoveled some fluffy eggs into his mouth. The room service breakfast was at their door at seven thirty-five. A guy could get used to this. No wonder Cam loved his job so much.

"Two water parks. About three hours each." Cam's leg rubbed his as he leaned forward to grab the tiny glass pepper shaker on the coffee table.

"Have fun."

"It's not a vacation."

Noah looked down at the dishes and silver lids and back

over at Cam. His T-shirt and shorts might have been emblazoned with the Havers logo, but they were still beach wear. Not that Noah needed to dress up for his job often, but he wasn't getting put up in hotels with room service either.

"What?" Cam said.

"You spend most of your time in hotels and at pools. Most people would call that a vacation."

"But it's good enough to take you to Hawaii."

"Because you fucking asked me." Noah set down his dish. "And I already paid for the ticket to LA, or we could just forget about it."

"I don't want to forget about it. I want to know why you suddenly have an issue with my job."

"I don't have an issue." Frustration burned the back of Noah's throat. Was this how it was going to be? If they weren't fucking, they were fighting?

"Then why did you say that last night?"

"We were fighting. You don't ever say stupid hurtful shit in the middle of a fight?"

"I don't know. You're the only person I've fought with who I've bothered to actually listen to since I left home." Cam had his glasses on again. They made his eyes look even greener and sexier than his contacts. Right now they were wide open in an expression without a trace of Cam's usual self-assurance.

Noah took a deep breath. He'd already spilled his guts for Cam's inspection last night. How much stupider could Noah sound? "I don't have an issue with your job," he repeated. "I just wish I could see you more often."

Cam smiled and that I-got-what-you-want expression came back into his eyes. "I don't have to travel as much in the winter. Don't you get a semester break? You could come up and spend it with me."

"In January." Noah tried to get his tone as dry as possible, but Cam apparently wasn't listening that closely.

"Great. I'll be sure to keep my schedule clear."

Noah wanted to grab Cam's shoulders and pin him to the couch, force him to listen. *I'm in love with you, you idiot, and I don't want to keep living in two different states.* How could Cam not figure this out on his own? How could he decide they were what—dating, going out?—and then ignore the fact that at best they saw each other once a month? This wasn't going to work.

Cam gulped down some coffee and leaned over to kiss him. "I'll be back by three. Maybe we could go out tonight. If you want to go back to bed, just put the tray out in the hall." He kissed him again, deep enough for Noah to taste the coffee on Cam's tongue. He pushed the hair off Noah's forehead. "Really?" Cam asked again.

Noah rolled his eyes and sighed. "Really."

Cam winked. "Good."

Noah was left alone to remind himself that he'd come too many times in the last twelve hours for his dick to respond to something as silly as Cam's wink.

〰
〰

There was always plenty of work in Orlando, so Cameron had been to this bar more than a few times. Predictably, it was packed on a Saturday night, filled with sweat and smoke and hot moving bodies. Cameron surprised himself by settling a possessive hand at the small of Noah's back as soon as they cleared the door. If Noah minded, Cameron couldn't see it in the first smile he'd seen on Noah's face since last night.

Cameron had been thinking about that smile all day. Since Noah had told Cameron he loved him, Cameron couldn't seem to stop smiling, but he couldn't get one on Noah's face. He knew he hadn't given Noah the answer he wanted to hear, but Cameron just couldn't lie about it.

He thought about Noah when he wasn't around, wondered what Noah was doing, how he was. Was that being in love? Cameron had always thought that if he did fall in love, he'd know. It would be something that happened, not something that was simply there. Did you wake up in the morning and decide you were in love along with whether or not you wanted bacon?

Noah's shirt grew damp under Cameron's palm, but he didn't want to take his hand off him. Usually the only reason he went to a bar was to cruise. Tonight he was only going home with Noah. The only piece of ass he was interested in was already a few inches from his fingers. It was a weird feeling, but not as odd as the compression in his chest when he saw guys looking at Noah.

Noah was in a maroon T-shirt, so tight it looked like his biceps were going to tear through the sleeves, tight enough to see not only his pecs but his abs and even the line of his breastbone. Maybe all that attention was the reason he was smiling. *All this and he switches, too. But he's mine.*

"Want a drink?" he shouted in Noah's ear.

"Sure."

Dancing wasn't that easy. Noah was too big to tuck in against him or to curl up behind. They moved out of synch for a few beats, but when Cameron grabbed Noah's hips, Noah made himself fit, sliding a leg between Cameron's and bringing those big hands up to Cameron's shoulders. What really made it work was seeing Noah's dimples again. Cameron had missed them.

His tongue had missed them. His hands skated around to Noah's ass, and Noah arched into him. Oh yeah, this would work.

As Cameron made his way back from the bathroom, having turned down more than one offer of company, he picked Noah out of the crowd without difficulty. Even though Noah's back was to him, his height made his dark head easy to spot. Cameron stepped around some guys to come up right behind Noah, wondering what he'd do if Cameron just went up and ground into his ass. Cameron stopped and changed his plans when he heard Noah's deep voice.

"No thanks. I'm with someone."

"Oh yeah. I saw him."

The guy leaning into Noah was gorgeous—and probably not a day over twenty-two. His long, curly, light brown hair framed a face like an angel in one of those Renaissance paintings. Those perfect bow-shaped lips were damned close to Noah's.

Maybe Noah was blocking the other guy's view of Cameron standing silently behind them, because the guy wouldn't suggest anything with Cameron standing right there, would he?

"What about the three of us? You can fuck me while your boyfriend fucks you."

The thought sent a flush of heat through Cameron's body.

"Sounds great, but we're...exclusive."

Cameron could hear the smile in Noah's voice and wanted to cover those dimples before threesome guy got overwhelmed by the sight of them.

"Now that is a shame."

The guy leaned in. Cameron couldn't see around Noah's shoulders, which was probably a good thing, because Cameron bet the jackass was probably kissing *his* boyfriend. He took a step forward, but the guy disappeared into the crowd.

"Who was that?" Cameron's hand slid onto the small of Noah's back again, cradling the dip above his ass.

"Gordon." Noah turned and smiled at him.

Cameron wanted to lap tequila from those dimples.

"He had an interesting idea, but I told him I was busy," Noah said, his smile deepening to flash his teeth.

"What was his idea?"

"Why? Do you want me to call him back?"

Cameron licked his lips. "No. I'm pretty sure I can come up with a few interesting ideas on my own."

"Yeah?" Noah had a look on his face that made Cameron wish it wasn't going to take half an hour to get back to their hotel.

Cameron pulled Noah's head down to kiss him. Noah smiled right into Cameron's mouth as his tongue teased at those curved lips. Tightening his grip in Noah's hair, Cameron pressed closer, hand cupping Noah's ass.

"I'm too old to get off in a bar," Noah murmured against Cameron's mouth. "Let's go."

Cameron caught Noah's shoulder as he turned toward the door. "You're okay with this? With not fucking other guys?"

Noah's smile went away. "How the hell can you ask that? I told you—"

Cameron pulled Noah's head down again. "And I heard you. I'm sorry, I'm just—"

Noah's mouth opened under his, wet and slick, pressing back hard.

When they stopped for breath, Cameron whispered, "Listen, Noah, I just don't want you to think that you can't do anything,

I mean if you want to dance or whatever with other guys."

"Just don't fuck them? Is that what we're talking about?" Noah grabbed Cameron's chin.

Once during training someone had practiced the Heimlich maneuver on Cameron with real-life force. It had taken his diaphragm a good minute to start working again on its own. This felt worse. Noah's unexpected anger hit his gut almost as hard as that two-fisted thrust. Cameron tried to move his head, but Noah's grip was too tight.

"You just what?" Noah went on. "Want to be able to fuck without rubbers, is that it? Just stay clean and that's all that matters?"

That was part of the reason—the reason he'd mentioned it in the first place—but being at this bar had reminded him how much he didn't want anyone but Noah.

Noah released his chin. Cameron stopped himself from rubbing away a trace of soreness as Noah backed away from him.

"Where are you going?"

"To dance."

Cameron finally caught his breath before following Noah to the edge of the dance floor. Apparently, Noah'd had no trouble finding a dance partner. It wasn't Gordon, but it didn't seem like there was anyone who wasn't hot there tonight. Cameron had just found them when Noah started grinding hips with random dancing guy. Cameron couldn't even get a good look at the guy's face because Noah's shirt rode up in the back, exposing the way his spine dipped right above his ass.

If that guy's hand found it...and then it did, sliding under Noah's shirt, when there was barely enough room in there for Noah. Under the strobing lights, the guy's hand looked stark white against Noah's tan. The hand would look a lot better if

Cameron broke every bone in it.

Cameron gripped the beam next to him to keep from stomping out there and ripping that hand away. The part of his brain that knew this was what Noah wanted, that he was deliberately trying to piss Cameron off for some reason, was losing control to the part that didn't care, that only knew that Noah was getting felt up by a hand that wasn't his.

Just one dance. Cameron could last one dance. He'd tell Noah he'd made his point, that yes, Cameron got jealous when he watched Noah dance with someone else like he wanted to fuck that someone else. But when the guy's hand that wasn't up Noah's shirt curved down over Noah's ass, fucking lifted under Noah's ass and squeezed...Cameron had no intention of moving, but suddenly he was standing right next to Noah and his new friend.

"Having fun, babe?"

"Uh-huh."

Sheer force of will kept Cameron's hands tucked in the back pockets of his jeans. "How much more fun you plan on having? I know you're on vacation, but I've got work tomorrow."

Noah turned in the guy's arms so he was actually rubbing his ass against the guy's crotch. "You said you didn't care if I wanted to dance."

Cameron didn't like to make scenes, but he hadn't gotten this far in his life by just watching things go by. He grabbed Noah above his elbow and yanked him forward. "Point taken," he growled in his ear, and then kissed him as hard as he dared without splitting their lips.

Noah let Cameron pull him toward the door, which was fortunate since Cameron hadn't planned out what he'd do if Noah actually resisted. Cameron wanted to shove Noah into his rental car like it was some kind of movie scene, but as soon as they cleared the door of the bar, Cameron let go of Noah's arm and kept on walking. They'd both made their points. Noah could follow or he could get a fucking cab.

Noah followed, his long legs catching him up until they were walking next to each other, but not with each other.

Cam didn't say a single word on the way back to the hotel. Noah's own anger had evaporated as soon as Cam pulled him away from the guy Noah had been dancing with. He wondered if he'd finally pushed Cam too far. He looked over at the tight set of Cam's jaw. Maybe Noah had finally pushed Cam far enough.

Arousal had been pumping in Noah since he'd danced with Cam, a deeper thrum than the one he always got around Cam. Now as he thought about that kiss, wondered exactly what was going to happen when they were alone in the hotel room, his cock filled and thickened in his jeans until he had to shift in the seat.

Cam glanced over, but didn't say a word. Noah's dick got harder, throbbing with its own pulse. The tension should have made him uncomfortable, but all it was doing was making him so hard he wanted to rub himself to take the edge off.

He wiped his sweating hands on the thighs of his jeans, and the shift of the seam against his dick made him bite his lip.

"Don't even think about it." Cam's voice wasn't much above a whisper, but it was still loud in the car.

Neither of them said another word until they got into the room. Noah waited for an explosion that never came. Cam put the keycard on the dresser, took his wallet out of his jeans, started on his contacts. Bewildered, Noah took his own wallet and keys out of his pocket. He moved to put them on top of the dresser next to Cam's, and Cam was there.

He never touched him with his hands, just crowded him

157

back against the wall. Noah slid down until he matched Cam's height, and Cam put his hands on the wall above Noah's shoulders. There was still a breath of space between them.

"I want to know what that was about." Cam was still pissed. Good. Noah breathed in Cam's anger like a drug. If this was all the emotion Noah could get out of Cam, he'd take it.

Noah shrugged.

Cam's hand threaded into Noah's hair, twisted hard around the handful. "You wanted my attention, you got it. You wanted to know if I get jealous, I do." His voice deepened to a growl that would have gotten Noah hard on the spot if he weren't already about to pop the button on his fly. "If that was all you wanted, Noah, you'd better tell me. Because otherwise I'm gonna think there's something else you're looking for." He yanked that strand of hair.

Noah swallowed hard. Shit. Where the hell had this come from? He'd made it twenty-six years without wanting anyone to control him like this. He wondered if he wanted Cam to actually hurt him.

"Yes."

"Yes, what?"

"I want—" Noah couldn't figure out how to tell Cam. "Do it."

Cam nodded and stepped back, turning them so his own back was to the wall. His hands pushed Noah's shoulders, and Noah went to his knees.

Noah rubbed Cam's dick once before pulling him free, finding Cam just as hard as Noah was. His throat spilled out groans before he even got Cam clear of his fly. Noah licked him, quick and teasing around the head, a long, soft lick up the shaft.

Cam's hand tangled in Noah's hair again, yanking hard

enough to sting. "Suck it down. Take it all."

Noah filled his mouth with spit and stretched his lips wide. Cam's hips pumped as Noah took Cam in, forcing himself to the back of Noah's throat. He tried to catch his breath, but Cam stayed deep, swiveling his hips, and it was all Noah could do to keep his teeth covered. Cam eased back long enough for Noah to catch a breath and then he was back, dragging Noah down around him.

Noah's world was nothing but that cock in his mouth, jammed into his throat. He tried to use his tongue, to swallow around him, but Cam wouldn't let Noah set the pace. He breathed as much as he could, spit running down his chin. He got his hands on the shaft, stroking as Cam shifted Noah's head back and forth, and then he got caught in the rhythm Cam had set, throat opening, stretching, so that Noah could get down around Cam's dick.

"That's it. Every inch."

Noah could barely hear him. He had no sense of time, his mind on nothing but how to get that cock deeper into his throat, to ease the pressure on his jaw. Cam pulled back for a second, and Noah lifted Cam's balls to his mouth, jaw so open Noah could get both in. His hand worked the skin of Cam's dick while rolling them over his tongue, jerking Cam fast and hard.

Noah ducked underneath to tongue the salty, smooth skin of Cam's perineum, pressing hard when Cam groaned and spread his legs wider. Noah stretched his neck, but he still couldn't reach all the way back.

Cam slapped his dick into Noah's cheek. "Don't forget what you're down there for."

Noah lifted his head and swirled his tongue around and under the rim before he slid back down to the root. It was easier now that he'd caught his breath, easier now with Cam groaning, his hand gone soft in Noah's hair. He let Cam rub against the back of Noah's throat before relaxing the muscle and swallowing him in. He'd just found a rhythm that had Cam gasping when Cam pulled him off. Noah sucked hard on the tip as it slid from his mouth.

"Fuck." The word might have been ripped from Cam's guts. He looked down at Noah and breathed fast and even. "Still with me?"

Noah nodded.

"Good because I think you need to know what I think about you rubbing your ass on another guy's dick."

"It wasn't—"

Cam's thumb over Noah's lips stopped his denial—which had been pointless to begin with. Two layers of denim hadn't been enough of a barrier to keep Noah from feeling the thick length of his dance partner rubbing right in the crease of his ass.

"Get the lube and a rubber. And get your clothes off."

Noah dug the stuff out of the nightstand and turned back. Cam had ripped off his shirt but kept his jeans on as he sat in the wheeled desk chair.

Noah toed off his sneakers. His fingers were shaking a little as he popped the buttons on his fly. Whether because he was nervous or just too fucking turned on to think straight, he wasn't sure. He just knew it took him way too long to get his jeans off his legs and kicked away with his socks.

"Get me ready to fuck you."

Noah reminded himself that this was what he was asking for, knew if he said he was uncomfortable, Cam would stop. But Noah didn't want Cam to stop. Something inside Noah wanted this, wanted to let Cam control everything, to push until Noah broke, shuddering and fucked limp.

He knelt and lubed the head of Cam's dick before ripping open the condom wrapper. Cam watched through heavy-lidded eyes. Noah wanted to do something that would make Cam take more notice. Rolling the tip of the condom on, Noah got his mouth over the bitter latex and pushed it down the rest of the way with his lips. Cam bucked once into Noah's throat, and the rubber taste had him gagging the way even the worst pressure of Cam fucking his mouth hadn't.

"Noah…"

There was a threat and warning in that growl, but Noah couldn't figure out what he'd done wrong.

"Hand me the lube and turn around." Cam pushed his legs open until he was straddling the chair.

Noah's heart and lungs crowded up into his throat, forcing a thin sound out of him when Cam traced his crack with a slick thumb. The lightest press of his thumb inside him, just enough to make his nerves sing, and then Cam's hand was on his hips, guiding him down and back.

"Hold on to the desk."

"Cam—" The head of Cam's dick felt huge against Noah's ass. His body wasn't ready for this.

Cam gripped Noah's hips, pulling him back. The head popped past the first tight ring. Noah's thighs strained to hold him up against Cam tugging him back, forcing his way inside Noah's body.

He swallowed back the *Wait!* burning on his tongue. Just as Cam pushed past the second ring, Noah's legs started to tremble.

"Just sit back." Cam's thumb dug into Noah's hipbone. "You wanted it, begged for it, dancing like that. Now you're going to take it. Push yourself onto my cock."

Cam's words floating in Noah's head relaxed him like a hand on his dick, and he let himself go until his thighs hit Cam's, the muscles still so tight Noah could feel every twitch and pulse in Cam's dick.

"Hold on," Cam warned.

Cam rolled him with the momentum of the chair. Both Cam's hands were on Noah's hips now, lifting him as Cam pushed himself back and forth, scraping inside, brushfire on Noah's nerves. His fingers squeezed the desk so hard he thought he'd splinter it.

"C'mon, babe. Move with me."

Noah couldn't breathe without a million volts tearing up through his spine. How was he supposed to move? He groaned.

"Fine." Cam wrapped an arm around Noah's waist and tipped him forward over the desk.

Noah reached out for balance as Cam took three long, deep strokes and started fucking like a jackhammer. His hand squeezed Noah's ass, pulling him wider.

"Gonna feel me all day tomorrow. Gonna feel me if you think about dancing like that again." Cam's teeth sucked a bruise into the skin between his neck and shoulder that Noah barely felt. His fingers scrambled for the far edge of the desk to brace him against Cam's hard thrusts, knowing better than to reach for his cock.

"That's it. Fuck back into me. So good, babe," Cam panted.

They were flying now. Bodies working fast, Cam's hips slamming like fists against Noah's ass, blunt counterpoint to the sharp sensation inside.

"Don't come. Don't you fucking come, Noah."

Noah could feel it waiting there under his skin, ready to

pop without even a touch on his dick. So close. He could come without shooting. But Cam would still know, could still feel it. Forcing it back was like trying to push away an ocean wave. Noah rode the fine edge between surrendering enough to let his body enjoy the fuck without losing enough control to come.

He didn't think Cam could fuck him harder until he did, until Noah had to let go of the desk before his fingers broke as they shoved it into the wall. His mouth stopped taking orders from his brain, and he wanted to cringe at the desperate begging spilling from his lips.

"Harder, please, wanna feel you for days, wanna die from it, please don't stop fucking me."

That big come simmered in his balls, Cam's last shove pushing Noah's dick against the edge of the desk. Noah's muscles tightened to hold it back, tightened around Cam, and Noah felt Cam swell thicker inside him.

"God, babe, so so..." and it was lost in Cam's choked groans as his hips jerked convulsively.

Noah's pulse hurt as it pounded in his denied cock, threaded cold fire into his balls, rippled the muscle of his ass on Cam's dick. Noah's breath sounded like a wind tunnel.

Cam eased out, the rubber slick and heavy against Noah's thigh. Noah reached for his own dick.

"No."

Noah's hand obeyed Cam instead of the demands of his body, slapping back down on the desk.

"Good boy."

That was almost the last straw. Noah was going to turn around and tell Cam he was done with this game. Ask what the fuck a guy had to do to get off around here. But Cam started jacking Noah, slow but steady. Nothing that was going to get him off in this century, but enough to ease the ache. Then Cam slipped two fingers past his swollen rim and pressed down inside, and Noah took off, bucking into Cam's fist, back onto those fingers. Cam curled them, fucked them in and out, drove back in with three, splitting him wide.

He pressed down in small, hard circles.

"There, fuck, please right there. God, yeah, please, I—"

"Now," Cam ordered.

Noah reached for it, suddenly afraid he couldn't—wouldn't—go after holding it so long. Cam's hand twisted around the crown, thumb pressing over the slit before going back to that sweet, hard rub. Noah shook, pinned down by a terrible press of sensation, so good there wasn't room for it inside him anymore and everything lined up to trigger that first shot, a cascade of spasms flowing out of him, bursting as his nerves shredded like confetti.

♒

Noah woke in the middle of the night, body still buzzing from coming so hard. Cam had all the pillows again, so Noah dropped his head onto hard shoulder.

Cam's eyes opened.

"Stole all the pillows," Noah explained.

Cam didn't offer to shift, so Noah made himself comfortable on Cam's chest.

Cam's hand stroked down Noah's back, pausing just above his ass. "How are you feeling?"

Noah's ass throbbed like something was still in him. "Fucked."

Cam's chest rumbled under his ear. "Good."

Far off down the hall, Noah heard the elevator ding. He knew Cam was still awake, could feel the awareness in his body. "Don't you have work tomorrow?"

"Do you have a point?"

Noah ran his hand down Cam's hip to where his dick swelled against Noah's side.

"That's an interesting point," Cam agreed on a low sigh. "Think you can get up for it?"

Noah didn't think his ass was up for another round, but his mouth could be. His jaw only ached a little. "Maybe."

"Maybe?" Cam shifted onto his side and kissed his jaw and neck.

The stir in his blood made Noah even more aware of how well-pounded his ass was. "Depends."

"Oh." Cam's smile made Noah horny and embarrassed at the same time.

"What if I said I wanted you to fuck me?"

Cam's suggestion definitely got Noah interested. But he didn't want Cam thinking he owed Noah anything. Cam hadn't done anything Noah hadn't wanted.

"Why?"

"Because it's going to feel good."

Noah could hear that there was something more. He rolled Cam under him, and Cam's legs dropped open, cradling Noah against Cam's stiff cock. Noah licked the notch in Cam's collarbone. "And?"

"It's going to feel even better knowing you can still feel me in your ass."

That made Noah jerk forward, his cock suddenly very ready

to play again. "Got a preference for how?"

"This is working for me."

"Did you put the stuff back in the nightstand?" Noah dimly remembered Cam wiping the come off them before helping Noah to bed. As soon as he hit the mattress, he'd been out.

"Yes." The s was drawn out since Noah was sucking hard on one of Cam's nipples, grazing it with his teeth.

"Okay." Noah got up on his knees and lifted Cam's ass off the bed.

"What are you—?"

Noah wasn't about to let this opportunity go. He buried his face in Cam's ass, licking, feeling the twitch of muscles as Noah circled the hole. He breathed in Cam's sweat and musk, the taste of that soft puckered skin sharp on his tongue.

"Holy shit." Cam's voice was a whisper, like he thought if he spoke too loud Noah would stop.

But Noah wasn't going to stop until Cam was wet and open enough to let Noah's tongue fuck him, until Cam squirmed and begged.

Cam's breath came in quick pants. Noah licked up to his balls, using the flat of his tongue to wrap around the sac before he went back down, pulling Cam's cheeks apart so he could wriggle the tip of his tongue inside.

Cam softened in his hands, legs dropping wider, body opening, and Noah pressed in deeper, groaning, kissing, sucking until Cam squeezed Noah's shoulder to get his attention.

"Fuck me, Noah."

Those words rolled right down Noah's dick, making it leak from the tip. The more his dick filled with blood, the more his ass throbbed.

He dove for the nightstand drawer. Lubing his sheathed dick with one hand, he stretched Cam with two fingers of the other, watching his face until the tension gave way to need, easy enough to read even in the dark.

Noah went into him slowly, holding tight to the root as that first constriction threatened to push him over the edge before he'd even started. He stroked a hand down Cam's chest, let Cam work himself forward and down.

Cam's hand tugged on his cock, slow short strokes, and he nodded. Noah arched his back and slid home. Cam's head dropped back against his pile of pillows, hand working harder on his dick.

Noah bit his tongue to keep from pleading with Cam to let him move. This wasn't Noah's first time, he could wait, but the feel of smooth, hot pressure all over his dick, the feel of Cam—fuck—*Cam* tightening and shifting around him was going to make Noah lose his mind.

"Go," Cam whispered.

Noah started slow, but Cam rocked to meet each stroke and Noah couldn't keep it back.

Cam hiked his legs up and dragged Noah down. "Tell me."

"Feel you in me. Every time I fuck into you, damn it." The flex of his own muscles made Noah feel like he had a good-sized plug in his ass.

Cam's head dropped back again, and Noah arched up, pinning Cam's thighs wide as he fucked him fast. Cam's ass dragged against Noah's thrusts, the hot muscle working him until he felt his balls fill.

He should have been able to go longer, God, he'd just come hard enough to turn his dick inside out, but it was there. His hips went into overdrive. The second before he lost it he heard those sweet groans in Cam's throat, and let it go, let Cam's muscles squeeze him right over the edge as Cam shot over his belly and chest. Noah was too tired to do more than tie off the rubber before he dropped it on the floor and hand Cam his T-shirt from the side of the bed.

Noah collapsed on top of Cam.

"Jesus, Noah, you need to get in shape. You're only twenty-six."

"Fuck you."

The rumble of Cam's chest under Noah's ear sent him right to sleep.

Chapter Nine

Cameron spotted Noah in the rows of blue seats at Gate 43A of LAX. It had been eight weeks since Orlando, eight weeks since Cameron had been able to have more of Noah than just his voice on the phone. Cameron'd had a lot on his plate, end-of-the-year paperwork, meetings, evaluations, reviews. But in spite of all the work to keep him busy, he'd spent a lot of time missing Noah. Talking on the phone, even fucking over the phone, was a piss-poor substitute.

Noah pushed up out of his seat as he approached, and Cameron spent a second simply looking before pulling Noah in for a long, hard hug. The smell of Noah's skin kept Cameron glued to Noah's neck for longer than was smart in the middle of an airport, but Cameron didn't know until he pressed his nose there how much he'd missed it.

He wanted to haul Noah off into the bathroom and kiss him until he made one of those whimpers that Cameron had been listening to on the phone for six weeks, but since they could kick you off a plane for sneezing these days Cameron only took the seat next to Noah and squeezed his hand.

Noah's dimples cut deep into his tanned cheeks. "I missed you, too."

As they settled into their seats for the flight to Hawaii, Cameron didn't know how he was going to get through these next five hours with Noah next to him and not touch him. Cameron had offered Noah the window seat, and they pulled up the armrest between them for extra room. Noah was warm against Cameron's side, shoulders and arm hard against him, and then Noah had to go and hook his bare ankle around Cameron's.

Maybe making plans to go parasailing this afternoon had been a mistake. They'd booked a couple of activities ahead of time for whenever Cameron wasn't busy with the conference. He'd wanted to show Noah everything he loved about Hawaii. Noah might have grown up in Florida but there was nothing like Hawaii. Now, with Noah all warm and smelling so damned good next to him, he wanted to fuck him as soon as they landed and then go parasailing. With other guys, he'd always wanted to fuck them and then get back to work, go off to another place, but with Noah...

He wanted to show him things, wanted to learn golf with him, wanted to fuck him and get fucked and wake up and do it all over again. They got tiny bottles of water from the stewardess, and Noah shifted his arm until they could lean comfortably together without doing anything that would get them kicked off the plane thirty thousand feet above the Pacific.

"Be sure to move your legs around," Cameron murmured in Noah's ear.

"Don't get kinky with me on the plane, Cam. I'm having a *hard* enough time."

Cameron choked on his water, and Noah flashed his dimples at him.

"Seriously, though, your legs can swell."

Noah looked at him and burst out laughing. "My legs?"

"Shut up. Go to sleep."

Noah's knuckles rubbed against his thigh. "We'll see what

swells."

"Don't be a brat." God, Cameron should have jerked off in the shower this morning. If the plane got in on time and they got picked up on time, they'd have two hours before their parasailing reservation.

He pitched his voice to a growl in Noah's ear. "Keep it up, babe. Payback's a bitch. You'll spend the whole week walking funny."

That weekend in Orlando had become Cameron's favorite jerk-off fantasy. Noah's too, if the hitch in his breathing and the way he shifted his shorts down was any indication. Noah caught his eye and managed to make drinking from his water bottle look absolutely obscene.

It was going to be a long flight.

〜〜
〜〜

The first day of presentations left Cameron's brain numb, but Noah's enthusiasm dragged Cameron out of the hotel room to show him everywhere Noah had been during the day. They ended the evening walking a few miles down the beach to have a barefoot dinner in a place that Noah swore served the best conch soup he'd ever had.

"Cam, this sand really is black. Like crushed onyx or something."

It was about the ninth time Noah had mentioned it and his voice was still full of wonder. Noah bent down and came back up with a handful, staring at it in the starlight.

"We'll bring a jar home."

Noah tossed the handful at his chest. "You laughing at me, Lewis?"

Cameron hadn't been, had just wanted to hold on to a piece of the enthusiasm vibrating off Noah's skin, but the challenge in his voice was irresistible.

"What if I am?" Cameron jogged a couple of steps backward.

Noah launched himself at Cameron's legs and they went down on the gritty sand. "Gonna make you eat it."

"Hmmm. Sounds like fun."

Noah pinned his shoulders down. "Eating sand?"

Cameron lifted his head to kiss him, laughing into his lips. He loved the way Noah made him feel. His head dropped back onto the sand, body thumping with an awareness and energy that stole his breath. He loved Noah. All this time. What the hell had Cameron thought this was?

Noah's face got serious, and his hands left Cameron's shoulders. "Cam?"

Cameron even loved that stupid nickname when Noah said it. Reaching up, Cameron pulled Noah for a kiss, ignoring the grit of sand on his lips. Noah's hands settled on Cameron's hips, his thumbs brushing the skin where his shirt rode up.

Voices floated down from the path above the beach, and Noah raised his head. "Room?"

"Room," Cameron agreed.

They kissed in the empty elevator, sand sifting out of Noah's hair when Cameron stroked his fingers through it.

They kissed in front of their door, while Cameron reached behind him to slide the card through the slot.

It took three tries with Noah's tongue stroking in Cameron's mouth sending hot, slick sensation down to his dick, but then they were in their room and their clothes hit the floor. Cameron's heart and head pounded from more than the sensation of Noah licking inside his lips. Cameron was about to fuck the man he loved, and it felt like the first time and it felt so familiar. The back of his knees hit the bed, and Noah fell on top of him.

Cameron hauled his breath back to him in desperate lungfuls. Noah was already licking the inside of Cameron's thigh and back up the groove to mouth his hip. Noah went back down the other side, lips hungry on Cameron's skin. Noah kissed Cameron's cock, the side, the head, sliding down with long licks before wrapping his tongue around his balls. Cameron felt Noah's smile as he took Cameron into his mouth and watched the dimples disappear as Noah's cheeks hollowed with suction.

Cameron's body burned with the need to touch Noah even if it meant giving up that soft, wet mouth. He hooked Noah's arms and dragged him up.

Their dicks slid against each other as they kissed. Cameron tasted the salt of his skin on Noah's tongue while it stroked along his until it was lost in the taste of them together.

"Want to suck you," Noah murmured against Cameron's lips.

"Me too."

Noah turned around and shifted on his side so they could sixty-nine before diving back on Cameron's dick. Wet heat surrounded his cock as the satin-slick weight of Noah's cock filled Cameron's mouth. He bobbed until he heard Noah groan in frustration. Noah pushed Cameron onto his back and straddled his body.

"What?"

"Can't get down far enough like that." Noah braced his hands outside Cameron's thighs and took him down to the root. Sensation rolled up his spine, sending him bucking up against

173

Noah's ass. He pulled it down against his mouth, trying to pour out the pleasure Noah was giving him back into his body.

Noah's lips tightened as he sucked up the length of Cameron's cock, soft and loose on the downstroke. Cameron slid his hand between them so he could jack Noah's dick while tonguing his hole.

Cameron's dick popped free of Noah's mouth. "Don't. Gonna come," Noah pleaded.

"That's the plan."

And then as Noah licked and sucked at Cameron's balls, he thought of a better one. He slapped blindly at the nightstand, found the lube and a condom and lifted his head.

"Turn around."

Noah gave a last long suck on Cameron's dick before complying. Straddling his chest, Noah looked down into Cameron's face, hair almost covering those bright blue eyes. Noah reached up and brushed it back before grabbing the lube and reaching behind himself.

Cameron's gut clenched watching Noah's face shift as he slicked and stretched himself on his fingers. Cameron wanted to take over, but his coordination was shot and it took him a minute to remember how to move his muscles. Noah took the condom from Cameron's shaking fingers and rolled it down.

"Check it," he muttered, and Noah turned to look behind him.

"We're good." Noah smiled as he scooted his hips back.

"Don't go too far."

"Huh?"

Cameron curled his head up and pulled the tip of Noah's dick in his mouth.

"Oh. God." The depth of Noah's groan meant he'd figured

out Cameron's plan.

"Put me in you."

Noah's hands shook a bit, but finally he managed to slide the head of Cameron's cock into his body. Noah rocked back and then forward into Cameron's waiting mouth and hands. Noah's thighs trembled and squeezed Cameron's ribs. Noah couldn't move much, and Cameron imagined what it would be like to be suspended between those two sensations, needing more of both, unwilling to give either up.

Curses spilled from Noah's mouth, several of them directed at Cameron. His abs burned with the strain of curling his head up, giving him even more reason to do his morning crunches. Noah cradled Cameron's head. He watched Noah ramp up, felt the tension gather in his balls, in the tightening of the skin sliding over his lips.

Cameron groaned encouragement, lapping at the salty splash of precome.

"Shit."

Cameron had never heard Noah's voice go that high. As Cameron rocked up around Noah to try to give him more cock in his ass, more wet heat on his dick, Noah jerked against Cameron's lips and pumped come across his face and into his throat.

He kissed the head until Noah softened, until the gasps had faded into slow breaths.

Noah rolled off. Cameron stripped the rubber and climbed on top, his cock riding the groove over Noah's hip. As Cameron held Noah's face between his hands, Noah's eyes opened. Cameron bucked against hard muscle and bone, finding enough sweat to slick the friction. Noah's hips rolled under him. Grinding and shifting, Cameron rode that big body, watching his lover's eyes until the force of his orgasm slammed his own shut. It just kept coming, splitting his dick with heat as he spilled again and again onto their bellies.

He gasped into Noah's neck, mouth sliding slack over his sweaty skin. Cameron lay there drained until Noah eased Cameron onto his side and went into the bathroom and came back with a washcloth.

"Thanks."

Noah stretched back out on the bed, close enough to touch, and propped his head on his hand. "What do you think we'll see on our dive tomorrow?"

"Anything but a Great White is fine with me."

"I hope we see a moray eel. I think they're cool."

"Do me a favor and don't touch it. I like having all of you intact." Cameron pulled Noah's hand out from under his head and kissed his palm. There wasn't going to be a better time to say it. "I love you."

Noah jerked his hand back. "Aren't you supposed to say that before you come?"

Noah's disbelief stung, but Cameron supposed he deserved it. It had taken him far too long to get here.

He rolled onto Noah's chest and cupped his head. "Noah. Look at me."

Noah's eyes fixed on his, and the vulnerability Cameron saw there tightened his chest until it was almost too hard to say it.

"I love you."

Noah's slow smile lifted the weight off Cameron's chest.

"'Bout fucking time."

"Brat."

Noah was still smiling when he kissed him.

~~~
~~~

"What are your plans for the rest of the month?" Cam's familiar question got Noah up and looking at the calendar.

He heard movement through the phone and tried to picture Cam in the apartment Noah had never seen. Did Cam talk while lying on his bed, sitting on his couch, standing in his kitchen? The sounds suggested he was moving something around.

"My mom and dad are doing Thanksgiving. You could come down for the weekend. They wouldn't mind you coming to dinner," Noah said.

"I have to be at work the day after. Mandatory meetings. I can't get out of it. All the trainers have to fly in for it."

Fly in for it. Which meant you didn't have to live in Raleigh, North Carolina to work directly for Havers. Noah pushed back the resentment. Cam had said he loved him. They'd work out the rest.

"What are you doing the weekend after?" Cam went on.

Noah was completely and totally free. With Cam in Raleigh and Noah in Tallahassee he couldn't get more free.

"I'm free."

"Great. Tickets are a lot cheaper then."

Noah heard the click of computer keys.

"Can you pick me up at eight twenty Thursday night?" Cam asked.

"Sure." Noah wrote it on the calendar hanging in the kitchen as if he'd need the reminder. He'd have the flight number committed to memory as soon as Cam gave it to him. "Hey, isn't your birthday in November?"

"Yeah. It's that Friday after Thanksgiving."

Noah's parents would kill him, but if he left Wednesday after work he could make it to Raleigh by midnight. Mom would get over it and Dad would get over it if Mom did. "I could drive up."

"I'll be busy all day. It'll just be boring for you. Tell you what." Cam's voice hit that deep growl. "You can give me my present that Thursday night."

"What do you want?"

"I'll let you figure it out."

Cam had Noah laughing and off the phone before he realized Cam hadn't given Noah a good reason for not coming up for the long weekend.

On the first weekend in December, he took Cam back to the Polish restaurant and out to the movies on Saturday. They saw two movies before they left the multiplex. Licking the misting rain and popcorn salt from his lips, Noah hit the remote unlock for his truck as they walked across the parking lot.

"Aren't there any good theaters in Raleigh?" Noah asked.

"I don't know. I hate to go to the movies alone. It feels weird."

"But you don't talk during the movie."

"I know. It just seems like something you should do with someone."

Noah blinked through the rain and watched the animated Christmas lights on the roof of the store across the lot. "What do you want for Christmas?"

Cam bumped his shoulder. "You tied to my bed for twenty-four hours."

It would be nice if I knew what your bed looked like. Noah thought again of the sturdy iron frame and the green sheets.

178

"I'll see what I can do."

They slid into the cab, and Noah started the engine.

"So what are your plans for Christmas?" Cam wiped his glasses on his shirt.

"Can't they be our plans?"

"Okay." Cam put his hand on Noah's thigh. "What are our plans?"

Noah flicked on the wipers. "My family is going to Adam's in Jacksonville."

Cam took his hand back.

"I want you to come. I want to spend Christmas with you." Noah tried not to sound like he was begging. But he was.

Cam was silent.

"Did you want to go to your parents' house?" Noah offered.

"It's not that."

"We could get a hotel. I just want to be there Christmas morning."

"How about if you drive up to my place after?" Cam wiped his glasses again and slipped them back on. "You'll be more than two hours closer."

Noah turned to face him. "Is it Adam?"

"No. I'm just not the holidays-with-the-family kind of guy."

"Is there some kind of past trauma I don't know about?" Noah tried to make his tone light.

"No. I like decorations. I like presents. I like the idea of you and me having time off together."

"So why can't you just put up with a family holiday for two days?" Noah was back to begging, but Cam didn't care.

"I just can't see me doing it. I'm sure your nephews are great, but kids get on my nerves."

179

How could Noah explain it to Cam, that having him there would make this real, more than just fuck-you-when-I-see-you. Having him there at Christmas would say they were together, that this was going someplace. "This is all I want for Christmas."

Cam put his hand on Noah's face. "Noah. Babe."

It was the first time Cam had called Noah *babe* outside of bed without any hint of teasing in his voice. Noah wished he could enjoy it.

Cam rubbed his thumb across Noah's lips. "I love you. But no. Drive up and see me the next day. Stay as long as you can."

Maybe Cam did know what Christmas together would mean which was why he'd told Noah no. He believed Cam when he said he loved him, and Noah trusted Cam to not screw around, but Noah needed more. Maybe Cam didn't want green sheets. An apartment. A life together. The question was, could Noah handle having half of what he'd always wanted?

He swung his arm around Cam's seat to back out of the spot.

It wasn't easy turning Noah down for anything, especially when he did that look through his bangs like that, but Cameron still wasn't giving in. Christmas at Adam's house wouldn't be the warm and fuzzy Norman Rockwell painting Noah thought it would be.

Cameron knew Noah's parents and his brother were all right with Noah being gay—and Cameron really didn't expect Adam to lay him out for corrupting his baby brother—but no matter what, it was going to be awkward. The holidays would just make it worse. The thought of going and doing what Cameron did best, being charming and smiling through tense silences and uncomfortable stares, left him with that hollow feeling that had plagued him at the beginning of the year, a feeling he hadn't had since...Noah.

Noah was entitled to some disappointment, and Cameron let the brat be pissy the whole way back to his apartment. When Noah moped his way into the bedroom, Cameron decided it was time to put a stop to it. The tense line of Noah's spine as he faced the wall made Cameron smile. Seduction was something he was damned good at, and he loved a challenge.

It took a little longer than he expected, but kisses and dirty promises in Noah's ear got him to roll over. Hands rubbing hard across his pecs got him kissing Cameron back deep enough that Cameron thought he might get off from nothing more than Noah's mouth and tongue and the slow grind of his hips. The tug of Noah's slick mouth on Cameron's tongue went straight to his dick.

There was his pushy bottom, grabbing at his hips, slamming their cocks together, legs dropping open around him.

"Now," Noah groaned into Cam's mouth.

When they were ready, Cameron decided to tease Noah, popping just the tip inside him, moving it side to side. Eyes squeezed shut, Noah fought the grip on his hips to get more, to get Cameron deeper.

"Son of a bitch," Noah said.

Sweat prickled Cameron's back as he resisted his cock's demand to plunge into that clinging heat. He wanted Noah out of his mind with wanting it, needed to see the desperation in his eyes, but Noah kept them screwed tight.

Finally, Cameron let go of Noah's hips, and Noah jammed himself forward and down onto Cameron's cock. One stroke and Noah's ass pulsed around Cameron's dick, whole body shaking. Cameron looked down to see clear fluid pump from Noah's cock.

"Did you just come?" Cameron wrapped his hand around

Noah's dick. The blood still pulsed in the veins, keeping it hard.

Noah opened his eyes. "Kind of. It's happened before like that a couple times."

"That's fucking hot." Cameron bit his lip as he held himself perfectly still inside. "Can you go again?"

"Oh yeah."

Cameron arched back and slammed forward into perfect friction, slick heat. "I can't—"

"So don't. It's good."

He pinned Noah's thighs wide and rode him, balls slapping as Cameron hit the limit of their bodies again and again. Noah fucked back just as hard, spine arching off the mattress, heels pressing down to drive him up onto Cameron's dick.

Cameron thought about switching positions, keeping them going longer, but he didn't want to miss a second of this, of them climbing together hard and fast. Noah had his face twisted away, and Cameron reached down to turn Noah into a kiss, hips rocking in tight circles.

Noah gasped and jerked away. His breath hitched and caught in his throat. "Just fuck me."

Cameron arched back up, and Noah swung his knees up to Cameron's shoulders, Noah's hand stroking his dick in time with Cameron's thrusts.

"Take it so good, babe. Love to fuck you."

The throaty whines in Noah's chest made Cameron's hips stutter.

"Don't stop. God, don't stop."

"I got you, babe." Cameron held Noah's legs as his hand blurred on his dick. Cameron's own heart thudded as he watched Noah come, creamy ropes this time, streaking across his fingers and belly.

Grabbing Noah's hand, Cameron brought it to his mouth, sucking in those long fingers, the bitter taste and the draw in his mouth pushing him over until he pumped so long and hard he thought he'd split the rubber from the weight of that load.

"Fuck, Noah." His body kept jerking long after his balls had emptied, like his nerves had set up some kind of feedback loop of shocky pleasure.

Noah freed his fingers from Cameron's mouth and reached down to hold the rubber. Cameron's head dropped low on his neck, sweat streaking along his hairline, trickling down his spine. His hands were so deep into the backs of Noah's thighs there might be a permanent imprint but Cameron couldn't work out the muscle control to move them yet.

"Fuck." He took a long shuddering breath.

Noah's eyes opened, a small smile on his lips. "Can't. Dead."

Cameron tried to be careful about disentangling them, but his muscles kept quivering. Noah winced as Cameron jerked free.

"Sorry."

"It's all right."

The bathroom across the hall might have been miles away. Noah flopped over on his side. Cameron stayed hunched until the gross feel of the condom got him moving off the bed. When he came back, Noah was still awake. He waved off the washcloth Cameron had brought.

Noah rolled off the bed. "I think you got lube everywhere. I'm gonna shower."

What had this guy with sudden edgy energy done with his fucked-out, sleepy Noah? "Shower in the morning."

Cameron wouldn't go so far as to say he wanted to cuddle,

but with the sweat cooling on his body and bone-melting satisfaction pressing him into the mattress, he wanted Noah's warmth and the prickle of stubble against Cameron's shoulder as he drifted off.

Noah went across the hall anyway. If he came back, it was after Cameron had fallen asleep.

$$\sim\!\!\sim\!\!\sim$$

Cameron woke to full sun, jolting up in panic. Had they slept past the time he needed to be at the airport? Noah wasn't next to him. Cameron checked his watch. Eight thirty. He still had more than an hour before he had to leave.

The cold pit in his stomach warned him before he even made it to the living room. When he caught sight of Noah sitting on the couch, waiting, the ache spread out into Cameron's thighs, icy cramps in his muscles. He'd known things were wrong when Noah wouldn't look at him last night, but his body had been so warm and willing Cameron had let it go.

Noah looked up. "This isn't going to work."

A flush of anger snapped through the chill. "Because I won't spend Christmas at your brother's? That's selfish and stupid."

Noah's lips tightened. "No. Because you don't want to be with me."

"What the fuck? Noah, I love you. This is crazy." Cameron shoved the coffee table out of the way and stood in front of him.

Noah had his hands on his thighs. Cameron looked down at the threads poking through the holes in Noah's jeans. He had his sneakers and his shirt on. Cameron's legs ached again.

"You love me, but you don't need me. You're perfectly

184

happy spending all that time away from me."

Cameron sat next to him. "Who told you that?"

"You. You live six hundred miles away from me. And it doesn't seem to bother you at all."

"Of course it bothers me. But it's my job." Cameron considered putting a hand over Noah's, wondered if touch could drag this conversation away from the mess Cameron could feel coming.

"A job you can only do if you live in Raleigh? You can't do the same traveling through the summer from a different airport like half the other trainers?"

"It's not that easy. I don't see you coming up to Raleigh all the time."

Noah's hands turned to fists on his knees. "Every time I offer, you tell me no. I don't even know where you live."

"What the fuck does that matter? Fucking hell, Noah, what do you want me to do?" Cameron got up and paced behind the couch. The cold had burned away, but it didn't hurt any less. When the anger was gone, he knew he'd be left feeling hollow again.

Noah turned to watch him. "I need you. I need you to be with me. And you don't."

"Bullshit. You're pouting because I won't go with you to Adam's."

Noah came up off the couch and faced Cameron across the back. "If you want to make it about that, fine. Tell me why you won't come."

"I told you."

"Yeah. Those were really sincere reasons. I'm totally convinced." Noah rolled his eyes in perfect brat form.

"Fuck you."

"Even more convincing." Noah came around the couch. "Look. I thought about this all last night."

Cameron looked closer. Noah's blue eyes were puffy and dull. He probably hadn't slept, probably hadn't even come back to bed after his shower.

"So that's it." Emptiness crawled like a spider into Cameron's belly. "Things are hard so you just give up?"

"I'm not giving up, I'm giving in. I don't want to fight. And I don't want to feel like this anymore." Noah stepped forward and opened the door. "I called someone to drive you to the airport. I just can't."

Noah was just going to walk out?

"So where does this leave us?"

"I don't know."

It was the hardest question Cameron had ever asked in his life. "Don't you love me?"

Noah swallowed and closed his eyes. "I do. And I thought it would be enough. But it isn't."

It wasn't fair to spring this on Cameron like this. He wasn't ready. Give him an hour and he'd have all kinds of reasons why they could make this work. But Noah was being a pissy fucking brat and the door was open and—

"Noah?"

"I love you, Cam. But I can't." Noah went out the door.

Cameron threw his stuff into his overnight bag and found the number for a cab. He wasn't going to wait for one of Noah's friends to show up and lecture him on why he was a fucking bastard for not going to some stupid family Christmas. He went outside to wait for the cab, unable to keep his gaze from the spot where Noah's truck should be.

Things needed a little work, so that was reason enough to

dump him? God, this was why Cameron had always avoided relationships. Investing time and energy and emotion into something so that someone else could fuck it up in five minutes or less.

Chapter Ten

Cameron's anger had faded by the time his plane landed in Raleigh. Instead all he could see was that look of exhaustion and pain on Noah's face, how hoarse and deep his voice had been when he'd said, "I can't."

Admitting it made Cameron want to punch something, but he had failed. He never failed. Never failed a test. Never failed to get the job. Never failed to get what he wanted. But somehow, he'd totally flunked Intro to Relationships and Noah 101.

How?

Noah loved him. He loved Noah. They had amazing sex. They had fun out of bed. They could talk for hours or sit in silence and watch a movie. What part of making a relationship work was Cameron missing? He wasn't stupid. He knew the distance was an issue, but if Noah had given Cameron a chance to catch his breath, he'd have worked something out.

It took him almost two weeks to figure out how he'd managed to fuck up something he'd just realized was the best part of his life. Saying *I love you* to Noah was a promise that Noah could trust Cameron to make Noah happy. And Cameron hadn't. Hadn't tried. It wasn't only going to Adam's—which Cameron could still do if Noah really wanted to—but Cameron had always figured that if he was happy, Noah was happy. Cameron knew what he could do to fix it. Now he needed to be sure Noah wanted Cameron to bother.

At least Noah took Cameron's call.

"Still pissed at me?"

Noah sighed. "I'm not mad. I was never mad."

"So you haven't fallen in love with someone else?"

"Don't be an asshole."

"See, you are pissed." God, Cameron loved that brat.

"Fine. I'm pissed."

"Can you give me a little time?"

"For what?" Noah's voice was so cold, Cameron could feel the ache in his bones again.

"To try and fix things."

"How long?"

Cameron put every ounce of charm he could into his voice, praying Noah could hear his smile the way he could always hear Noah's over the phone, because Cameron'd had two weeks to realize how fucking empty his life was without Noah in it. *Please, Noah.* "Till the end of the month? I'm going to fix this."

"All right. Till the end of the month."

〰〰

"You didn't eat much," Noah's mom said as he stood next to her and dried the dishes in his sister-in-law's kitchen.

Because I have a large Cameron Lewis-shaped worry chewing a hole in my stomach. He hadn't heard from him since that cryptic phone call. Maybe Cam had decided Noah was just too much work.

"I ate a lot. I'm saving room for turkey tomorrow."

His four-year-old nephew tore around the island and plowed into his mother's legs, effectively distracting her from more pointed questions.

Adam started in when they were putting together one of Fisher Price's more torturously complicated toys for one-year-old Robbie. "Everything okay?"

"Why?"

"You're holding the directions upside down," Adam pointed out.

"Like I can tell, they're in fucking Korean anyway."

"Noah."

Noah had thought his mother was far enough away. "Sorry," he said to his mom. Studying the picture on the box, Noah snapped two bulky pieces of plastic together. "Real men don't need directions anyway."

Adam lowered his voice. "Seriously, dude. You're fucking depressing to be around."

"Merry fucking Christmas to you too." Noah finally got the last piece of plastic out of the nest of wiry twist ties and plastic pull tabs and threw it at Adam's head.

"So what is it? Someone need his ass kicked?"

"I can handle my own ass kicking, thanks."

"That's about all I want to hear about you and asses, bro."

"You started it."

Needles fell off the tree onto the directions as their father came up and stood over them. "You boys need help with that?"

"We're good," Adam answered quickly.

Their dad went to take a bite of Santa's cookies. Mom and Maria had the stockings done. Their project was the last one.

Adam poked Noah with the screwdriver. "Lighten up, man.

Or I'm siccing Mom on you."

"I'm fine."

"Yeah, whatever. Hand me the batteries."

〜〜〜

When the phone rang on New Year's Eve, Noah grabbed it before he even checked the number. But it was only Joey.

"Tell me again why you aren't coming to my New Year's Eve party?"

"I want to stay in and watch football." The excuse sounded pathetic even to Noah's own ears.

"Nope. You're coming over if I have to send Mark over to pick you up. You've been sitting in your apartment like shit on a stick for three weeks. That's bad enough. And then I get a call from your mother."

"Fuck. My mother?"

"Do you realize what you just said, sweetheart? You're a therapist's wet dream."

Noah smashed the phone against his forehead. His life was a fucking train wreck and his mom was calling his ex-boyfriend. "Why did my mother call you?"

"She said you were the Grinch Who Stole Christmas and she wanted to see if I knew why."

"What did you tell her?"

"Are you asking if I told her that you had such a big fight with the man of your dreams that you called me to drive him to the airport because you couldn't stand to be in the same room with him for another five minutes? That you ran like a scared rabbit before you begged him to throw you some more scraps of affection?"

"Joey."

"I said I'd keep an eye on you. Your mom likes me. She thinks I was a catch."

Noah could just picture Joey's smug smile. "I didn't have the heart to tell her you left me."

"So what time will you be here?"

"I'm not coming."

"Fine. I'll send Mark over at nine. See you later." Joey hung up.

Noah looked at his watch. It didn't get much more "end of the month" than five o'clock on New Year's Eve.

His phone rang again.

If it was someone else telling him to cheer up he was going to throw the damned thing through a window.

"Yeah?"

"Hello."

Just Cam's voice made Noah's throat tighten. Noah didn't know what to say. It might be the last time he ever talked to Cam, but Noah still couldn't break the silence.

"Do you have any plans for tonight?" Cam said finally.

"My lover is six hundred miles away. Why the fuck would I have plans on New Year's Eve?"

"Good. Then maybe you could come out and help me."

"Huh?"

"Come outside and help me."

Noah looked out of the front window. Cam was standing in front of a silver Saturn, the windows all blocked with boxes. Already feeling under the influence of five cups of Joey's lethal punch, Noah dropped the phone and opened the door.

Cam was standing there. "So, Havers is fine with me telecommuting and traveling out of Tallahassee."

Noah pulled Cam into the apartment.

"Does that mean you're fine with it too?" Cam's quick smile was nothing like his usual confident grin.

"What is this?"

"Me fixing things?"

Noah stared and waited for his brain to catch up. Cameron's eyes were searching his face.

"I hope you're fine with it, because I just drove ten hours with the seat pushed forward, and I don't think I can cram myself back into the car until I unkink." Cameron licked his lips.

Cam was nervous.

Noah was terrified. "You did this for me?"

Cam reached out and grabbed Noah's hips, pulling him until they were an inch apart. "You know, that's what I thought. The whole time I was packing." Cam looked down and flattened his hands on Noah's hips. "It wasn't until I hit Savannah that I realized it was for me." Cam shook his head. "This has been the worst month of my life."

"Not exactly fun times for me either."

"You want to know if I need you? Fuck. I was ready to quit if they wouldn't let me move. Don't ever do that to me again."

"What?"

"Push me away."

"Sorry."

"So, do I have a place to stay?"

Noah grabbed Cam's head and kissed him.

~~
~~

When the doorbell rang at nine thirty, Cam was sucking on Noah's hip.

"Fucking hell." Noah squirmed out from under him.

"What's going on?"

Noah filled him in on Joey's threat.

"Shit on a stick, huh?"

"Joey's words, not mine," Noah said.

"Pretty much sums up my month."

The doorbell rang again. Noah leaned over the bed and found his jeans.

"So you were lying."

Noah's throat tightened. "What?"

"When I asked if you had plans."

"Not my plan." Noah stepped into the jeans.

"Good." Cam pulled Noah back onto the bed and pinned him down. "Because any plans you have for the rest of your life better fucking include me."

"Include fucking you?"

"That too."

The doorbell rang again.

"Let me up." Noah pushed on Cam's chest. "He won't go away."

"Do you want to go to that party?" Cam shifted onto his side.

"Hell no. I've got plans."

~~~

"What did you tell Adam?" Cameron leaned into the trunk and grabbed his bag. His gut was already telling him that this was a very bad idea.

Noah slung his own bag over his shoulder and grinned down at him. "Just that I wanted to come visit for the weekend. And could I bring someone."

Cameron stared into the trunk for a minute, then looked back up at the house. "Couldn't you have told Adam who you were bringing? Got him ready?"

"And miss the fun watching both of you?"

They started up the walk. "Did I know you were this evil when I moved in with you?"

"Yep." Noah stopped and faced him. "He's not going to punch you. Or freak."

Cameron shifted his bag to his left shoulder. He really didn't think Adam would do anything physical, but it wouldn't hurt to be ready. Cameron had only seen Adam once since the wedding. And now Adam was a dad and Cameron and Noah— "It's just going to be weird."

Noah's shrug was only half as infuriating as it should be. Noah pushed the bell and grabbed for the door handle.

The door swung open and it was too late.

"Hi, honey." Adam's wife was just the way Cameron remembered her, small, pretty and full of soft curves. She gave Noah a hug, juggling the toddler on her hip.

The kid fixed wary eyes on Cameron, as if warning him off.

Trust me, buddy, if it was up to me, I wouldn't be here.

"And—" Maria stopped, her welcoming smile shifting to one

195

of confusion and then surprised recognition. Cameron was in all the wedding pictures after all.

She looked from him to Noah.

Noah smiled. "You know Cam."

"Of course. It's good to see you again, Cameron." She gave him a quick hug. "Adam." There was an almost imperceptible shake of her head. "Adam's in the kitchen giving Jake his lunch."

"Uncle Noah." A small, sturdy kid bolted into the hall and slammed into Noah's knees.

Noah hoisted him easily. "Hey, Jake."

Jake shared his brother's suspicious eyes, but had better vocal skills. "Who are you?"

Cameron really wasn't ready to be Uncle Cam. God, he hoped Ashley never had kids.

"This is my friend Cameron. He's a friend of your daddy's, too. Actually," Noah's voice lowered to a dramatic whisper, "it's kind of a surprise for Daddy."

"Really?" Jake opened his mouth to bellow, and Noah slapped a hand over it.

"A secret surprise." Noah ignored the glares Cameron was aiming at that shaggy, stubborn head.

Maria smothered a laugh. "I think it will be."

Cameron wasn't surprised that Adam hadn't followed his son out from the kitchen. Havers trained them carefully in psychology—though they called it client interaction. By making them come to him, Adam was trying to establish dominance over Noah's boyfriend.

Fucking great. Adam hadn't changed a bit. He still had to be top dog.

Cameron had kept his bag over his shoulder, though Noah

had dropped his in the hall before he picked up his nephew.

Noah looked at the strap, and Cameron sighed as he lowered the bag to the floor.

"C'mon. Gotta have Daddy's surprise," Jake whispered in a volume just under a roar.

Noah bent to put his nephew on the floor and held the boy's arm when he would have dashed off.

"Let Uncle Noah go first." Maria's voice took on a layer of amusement. "With his surprise." She grabbed Jake's hand.

There were only fifteen steps between the hall and the kitchen, but Cameron was pretty sure he knew how condemned prisoners felt on that last trip. He reminded himself that Noah's family was very important to him, that meeting Adam again as his brother's lover was no reason to feel like an awkward adolescent. Cameron just hated being out of his depth at anything. This whole being-a-couple thing wasn't anything he'd spent time preparing for.

Adam was sitting at an island counter in the middle of the kitchen, focused on the newspaper in front of him, probably checking to see if his beloved Braves had made any preseason moves. If Cameron weren't sure it would make things worse, he'd have laughed out loud at Adam's ridiculous alpha-male display. Whatever Noah had said about bringing someone to visit had clearly made Adam feel he had to make an impression.

"Hey, bro." Adam slid off the stool as they came in. "And—" There was a flash of genuine surprise and excitement on Adam's face. "Hey, Cameron, how the hell you been? I haven't seen you in..." His voice trailed off.

Adam leveled a narrow-eyed stare at them both and then cuffed his brother hard on the back of the head.

"Ow." Noah rubbed his head.

Almost without conscious effort, Cameron stepped forward. "Hey—" He stopped and looked at Noah, who was glaring at his brother. "You know, I've been wanting to do that for awhile."

"Big brother privilege." Adam's voice was hard.

"Hello," Noah interrupted. "Bigger than both of you. Could kick both your asses from here to Sunday."

"Try it, bitch." Adam seemed far more pissed at his brother than he did at Cameron. "So." Adam leaned back against the island, still pushing the whole lord-of-the-castle agenda. There were a lot of questions in that one word.

Cameron wished he'd worn his glasses so he could slide them back up his nose. He didn't usually fidget, but he was itching for a place to put his hands, and if Adam didn't stop acting like some father in a 50's sitcom who'd caught his daughter necking on the couch, Cameron was going to find a place for his hands on his old friend's face.

"Yeah," Cameron said. *It's like that, man. I tried. But just look at him.*

"And it's serious?"

Cameron stuffed his hands in his back pockets. "It is."

Adam looked over at his brother. Noah's eyes were so full of pride and love and pure fucking joy that Cameron wanted to grab Noah and kiss him right the hell there and let Adam deck him.

Noah nodded at his brother.

"Okay then. But if either of you try to turn my sons into"— Adam paused, lips pursed in disgust—"Yankee fans, I'll kill you both."

Adam reached out and hauled first his surprised brother and then a completely stunned Cameron into a hug. As he uncomfortably returned Adam's back slapping, Cameron watched Maria peek around the corner. Jake, who seemed to have one speed—full throttle—barreled into the kitchen.

"Daddy, did you like Uncle Noah's surprise?"

"I've had—" Adam looked up at his brother and bit back what he'd started to say. "Yes, son, it was great."

The next time they visited Noah's nephews, Cameron planned to come prepared with a year's supply of energy drinks, just so he could try to keep up. Robbie could barely walk, but had no trouble climbing to precarious heights when you weren't looking—and sometimes even when you were. Jake seemed intent on showing Uncle Noah every single toy in his possession—an astonishing sum total, though knowing how much Adam's parents had showered him with affection, Cameron shouldn't be surprised that the first Winthrop grandchild lived like a prince.

By the time Maria led them down to the fold-out sofa in the basement, Cameron was exhausted. She started unfolding the sheets to make up the bed, but Noah stopped her.

"We can manage. Good night."

"Night, guys."

Adam thumped down the stairs a few minutes later.

"Did you tell Mom and Dad about"—Adam flicked a quick gaze at Cameron and then at the bed—"about this yet?" He waved a hand at the whole situation.

"No. Why?" Noah looked up from where he was tucking in a corner.

Adam shrugged. He glanced at the bed again and then at the ceiling. "I'll—uh—leave the upstairs door locked—and uh—the laundry room's down the hall." He pointed.

"Huh?" Noah straightened up and stared at his brother as if he'd lost his mind.

"Don't leave my wife with the sheets if you—uh—" Adam's face turned bright red—showier than Noah's blush since he wasn't as tanned.

Cameron snorted. "Don't worry about it."

"Okay." Adam pounded back up the stairs. The click of the lock echoed in the basement.

Noah sat on the bed. "Sorry, Cam, he didn't act that way when he met Joey."

Noah's utter idiocy about the whole thing would have been funny, if Cameron didn't feel as embarrassed as Adam. Noah couldn't understand how hard it was for Adam to adjust his world view to realize that the guy who'd spent fifteen years as almost an extra member of the Winthrop family was now fucking Adam's baby brother.

Noah lay back across the bed and rolled onto his stomach, looking up at Cameron. "Are you pissed?"

"No." And he wasn't—for the most part. Adam had taken it better than he might have in Adam's place. He knew it wasn't that they were gay; it would have been almost as uncomfortable if Cameron had been with Adam's sister. He just wished Noah would stop pushing.

"Then why aren't you in bed with me?"

Cameron opened his mouth to call Noah pushy, to tell him to back off, and then had to sit down. If Noah hadn't pushed, Cameron wouldn't have this, any of it. And not having Noah was the scariest thing he could think of—far worse than feeling a little embarrassed around Adam.

Cameron stretched out next to Noah, who crawled onto Cameron's lap. Noah slipped his hands under the edge of Cameron's polo shirt.

"Oh, no. We are not fucking in your brother's basement."

"Why not?" Noah shifted and rocked their hips together.

"It's a bad idea." Though the reasons why it was a bad idea were escaping Cameron's mind as his cock started taking an interest in Noah's motion.

"Why?" Noah asked again.

"Uh—" Cameron brought his hands up to Noah's hips, but those hands were under orders from Cameron's little head and weren't doing a thing to slow Noah's motion. "I didn't bring anything."

"I did." Noah flashed his dimples and Cameron was in way too deep, but he didn't want to save himself.

"Noah." Cameron meant it as a protest, but it came out as a gasped plea.

Noah leaned down and kissed him. "Thanks, Cam. I know you didn't want to come."

Cameron kissed him back until he could taste the whimpers in the back of Noah's throat. Cameron pressed back into the pillows and arched his neck. "So is there a thank-you blowjob in my future?"

"Could be a whole week of them."

"I love you, you know that?"

Noah grinned again. "Yeah, I do."

About the Author

K.A. Mitchell discovered the magic of writing at an early age when she learned that a carefully crayoned note of apology sent to the kitchen in a toy truck would earn her a reprieve from banishment to her room. Her career as a spin control artist was cut short when her family moved to a two-story house, and her trucks would not roll safely down the stairs. Around the same time, she decided that Chip and Ken made a much cuter couple than Ken and Barbie and was perplexed when invitations to play Barbie dropped off. An unnamed number of years later, she's happy to find other readers and writers who like to play in her world.

To learn more about K.A. Mitchell, please visit www.kamitchell.com. Send an email to K.A. Mitchell at authorKAMitchell@gmail.com.

*When his girlfriend demands he settle down and start a family,
Cole Winchester has some hard decisions to make. Marry
his girlfriend, or finally own up to his taboo
attraction to other men.*

Taboo Desires
© 2007 Amanda Young

Cole Winchester feels like a rat, boxed into a corner. Faced with the prospect of being trapped in a passionless marriage, he makes the hard choice to end his relationship.

A run in with an old friend on the beach, propels Cole's fantasies out into the open and forces him to confront his taboo desires. Before him, lies the choice of a lifetime—embrace his desire for another man and all the pitfalls that come along with it, or return to his girlfriend and live out the safe half-life he carved for himself.

Warning, this title contains the following: explicit sex, graphic language, and hot nekkid man-love.

Available now in ebook from Samhain Publishing.
*Taboo Desires also in print anthology Temperature's Rising
now available from Samhain Publishing.*

Enjoy the following excerpt from Taboo Desires...

Cole turned to find Eric right behind him, close enough to touch. Tension ratcheted up a notch, growing thick and palpable in the dark. His arms felt empty and longed to reach out, pull Eric to him.

"Sorry about the dark," he rambled nervously, while stepping around Eric. "I would turn on the lights, but by the time I get to the breaker box, we could be upstairs anyway."

Upstairs. Alone together. With a big comfy bed just waiting for us to make use of it. Cole gave himself a mental smack and, through determination alone, managed to keep his hands firmly at his sides.

Inviting Eric home with him was the equivalent of playing with fire. Oh, he'd noticed the sly glances the younger man had been shooting his way all night, seen him sporting wood more than once. And then that kiss—he didn't even want to think about what might have happened if he hadn't pulled away at the last second. He'd been so tempted to let Eric kiss him, to see what Eric's lips would feel like against his own.

Eric was interested, of that Cole didn't have any doubt. The real question was, was *he* interested? His cock shouted, "hell yeah", but the rest of him was torn. Eric was a cute guy, and they seemed to have a bit in common, but he didn't know if he was ready to take that next step, to go from fantasizing about being with a man to actually doing it. He could see him and Eric being friends, yes, but lovers? Oh, he wanted to fuck Eric, no doubt about that, but he wasn't sure if he could go through with it. Twenty-seven years of being conditioned to believe homosexuality was wrong stood a silent vigil between him and what he desired.

"This way," he said and headed for the private door leading up to his apartment. "Just follow behind me and I'll try not to steer you into a wall."

Eric's footsteps echoed on the stairs as he tagged along. "Yeah, that would be good. I'd hate to run my head into a wall and end up spending the night on your sofa."

Yep, Cole thought, that would be a tragedy. If Eric spent the night, he could think of a lot better places for him to spend time. Like sprawled out naked in bed, underneath him, or on top of him, or hell, even upside down would be okay.

Cole stopped on the last step and unlocked the door. Eric waited behind him, one step down. Any closer and Cole imagined he would feel the heat radiating off Eric's body, feel his hot breath on the small of his back. That instantly brought to mind a picture of Eric's pink tongue—the same one he'd coveted earlier in the night while it ran across Eric's pouty lower lip—peeking out to lick at the delicate skin of his lower back, drifting lower to explore territory no woman had ever touched. What would that bubble gum tongue feel like moving over his ass, licking, prodding his entrance?

The cheeks of his backside clenched in response to the taboo image. His pulse quickened and in the dark, silent corridor, he could hear the resonance of his own labored breathing. As he shoved open his door and reached a hand inside to feel for the light switch, he wondered if Eric had noticed it too.

His hand never made it to the light. Eric rushed him from behind and pushed him up against the wall opposite the open door. A hand wrapped around the back of his neck and pulled his head down.

"Fuck it. I may be way off base here, but I think you want this as much as I do," Eric whispered, hot puffs of breath caressing Cole's skin with every word.

Before he could utter a response, soft lips pressed against his, and a tongue slid over the seam of his mouth, coaxing him to open wide. His eyelids fell shut and his lips parted, allowing Eric in. The first touch of Eric's tongue gliding along his sent an electric current ricocheting through his body. He groaned and tilted his head, losing himself in the taste and texture of Eric's mouth.

His arms rose of their own will and wrapped around Eric's slim body, zeroing in on his firm little ass and pulling him closer. Their bodies flush, tongues dueling, Cole could feel everything. A hundred sensations hit him at once and short-circuited his senses. The whoosh of breath leaving Eric's body, the fast thump of blood rushing through his own ears, the ache of his balls drawing tight, the hard ridge of Eric's cock rubbing against his own through too many layers of clothes.

He wanted them naked. Now. Wanted to touch and taste with an intensity that should've frightened him, and probably would have if he'd been in the frame of mind to care right then. Luckily, he wasn't. He was too tired of all the bullshit, of hiding and pretending to be someone he wasn't. Though he wasn't sure why, Cole felt safe enough to let go and be himself around Eric. The only thing holding him back was himself, and for the first time ever, Cole was ready to ignore the persistent little whisper of his overactive conscience and throw caution to the wind for what he wanted. Nothing mattered but the man in his arms and the flame burning hotter between them.

Cole spun them around and pressed Eric's back to the wall. He sucked Eric's bottom lip into his mouth and nipped it, savoring the sweet whimper he got in response. His hands slid between their bodies and fumbled with the button of Eric's pants. The damn things were skin tight—he couldn't get them unfastened.

Eric shoved Cole's hands out of the way and undid them himself, yanking the front of his jeans open before going to work on Cole's. In a matter of seconds, Eric had both their cocks out, in his slender hand, and was rubbing them together. He leaned up on tiptoe, pressed his lips against Cole's and whispered, "Touch me."

LaVergne, TN USA
01 February 2010
171719LV00001B/112/P